CONTENTS

WE LIVE INSIDE YOUR EYES (I) 1
THE LAND OF SUNSHINE 8
TRAVELER 21
THE MANNEQUIN CHALLENGE 38
GO WARILY AFTER DARK 54
DOWN HERE WITH US 66
SANCTUARY 90
A WICKED THIRST 110
THE NO ONE: A RHYME 140
YOU HAVE NOTHING TO FEAR FROM ME 143
THE MONSTER UNDER THE BED 158
THE HOUSE ON ABIGAIL LANE 160
WE LIVE INSIDE YOUR EYES (II) 223
STORY NOTES 225
ABOUT THE AUTHOR 231

WE
LIVE
INSIDE
YOUR EYES

KEALAN PATRICK BURKE

We Live Inside Your Eyes
Kealan Patrick Burke

We Live Inside Your Eyes copyright © 2019 by Kealan Patrick Burke

Visit the author at www.kealanpatrickburke.com

All stories copyright © by Kealan Patrick Burke

"We Live Inside Your Eyes (I & II)" copyright © 2019. Appears here for the first time.

"The Land of Sunshine" copyright ©2015. First appeared in *Dark Screams V*, edited by Brian James Freeman & Richard Chizmar, Hydra/Random House.

"Traveler" copyright ©2017. First appeared in *Darkfuse Magazine*, edited by Shane Ryan Staley.

"The Mannequin Challenge" copyright ©2017. First appeared in *Halloween Carnival IV*, edited by Brian James Freeman, Hydra/Random House.

"Go Warily After Dark" copyright ©2017. First appeared in *Tales from the Lake Volume IV*, edited by Ben Eads, Crystal Lake Publishing.

"Down Here with Us" copyright ©2016. First appeared in *Tales of the Lost Citadel*, edited by C.A. Suleiman, Lost Citadel Productions.

"Sanctuary" copyright ©2017. First appeared in *Dark Cities*, edited by Christopher Golden, Titan Books.

"A Wicked Thirst" copyright ©2017. Originally appeared in *Garden of Fiends: Tales of Addiction Horror*, edited by Mark Matthews, Wicked Run Press.

"The No One: A Rhyme" copyright ©2019. Appears here for the first time.

"You Have Nothing to Fear from Me" copyright ©2019. Appears here for the first time

"The Monster Under the Bed" copyright ©2019. Appears here for the first time.

"The House on Abigail Lane" copyright ©2019. Appears here for the first time.

For the #Bookstagram community on IG, whose unbridled love and enthusiasm for books often reignites the candle for me on those long grey days in which the words don't come easy.

This, and all the others, are for you.

WE LIVE INSIDE YOUR EYES (I)

THE LAST TIME CHARLIE FELT SAFE WAS IN THE WOMB. Since then, he has struggled to find his place in the world and though he is only thirteen, he fears he never will. When he asks his mother why he is the way he is, she tells him he was early, whatever that means, and that now it's too late. She weeps when she says this, and Charlie leaves the room to avoid addressing her tears. Hidden in the pockets of the things that frighten him most is the realization that he doesn't like his mother. Once, he did, but she was different back then, full of love and light. Now she's a ghost playing at being alive, a faded sheet hung upon a coatrack, only there to ensure he doesn't become a ghost too. But her efforts are minimal. She puts plates of food before him at predetermined hours that are cold and bland, so most of the time he pantomimes satisfaction while tucking the gruel beneath his tongue. It makes him wish his dog hadn't died, but he did, and his insistence on staying dead is proof that wishes don't come true, no matter what the storybooks say.

Someday he hopes to write a story, but he doesn't yet know what it will be. There is little to inspire him within the dank grey walls of this house except thoughts of escape, and even those only go so far, for what is there beyond this house but rain and boys with ugly smiles.

He is lost and alone, with only the girl in the window across the street for company.

She's there every day. Sometimes she waves. Mostly she doesn't. She simply watches him or looks down upon the cracked asphalt cul-de-sac where the older boys play stickball. Those boys used to mock her and throw stones at her window until one of them, the cruelest one, disappeared. Now they pretend they don't see her. But Charlie sees her. He wishes he could see her closer but like his father says, wishes are wet sticks that will never start a fire.

Then one day he ducks his head beneath the curtain and props his elbows on the sill, ready for another long afternoon of watching and hoping but the girl whose name he doesn't know is not there to look back at him. Instead, she's at her front door, looking back inside, jaw moving as she delivers what appear to be harsh words to someone or something he can't see. And then she is outside and tugging the stubborn door shut behind her.

Charlie is paralyzed by indecision.

He knows if he wanted to, he could run, even though his legs are not very good and he is not very fast, but maybe they would get him close enough to talk to the girl, close enough to see the color of her eyes, close enough to know her as something more than a distant face in his lonely world. His mother may try to stop him, but she is weak too. She will limit her efforts to a cry. Perhaps she will be bold and come to the door, but by then he will be gone, and he knows she won't follow. They never go outside. Hardly anyone does anymore. It's too wet and too cold and the air makes people sick. Only the cruel are immune.

He steps away from the window and in his mind, he is already hurrying down the stairs. The reality, however, is much different. Knees shaking, he slowly puts one foot before the other, one arm braced against the wall for support. The wallpaper is damp and gives way, the painted flowers crumpling inward under his touch. He curses his infirmity and wills himself to move, move, faster, faster, but there is no strength from which to draw the fuel he needs to continue, and he collapses to the floor. The carpet smells of mold, but it is a smell to which he is accustomed, so it does not motivate him to rise.

"What are you doing?"

The words come to him from a throat clogged with phlegm. He does not raise his face to look at his father, because he does not like to see him. He hates that he is repulsed but hating doesn't change it.

"There is a girl outside."

"What is she to you?"

"Nothing yet, and she won't be if I don't try to see her."

"What if she doesn't want you to see her?"

"Then she should take away my eyes."

His father grunts and Charlie smells bitter smoke and the foul stink of a body eating itself to pieces from the inside out. His father's hands dig into his sides like plastic shovels, and with audible effort, he is hoisted back onto his feet.

"Go then. Don't be out there long enough to bring your mother to the door."

Charlie nods his acknowledgment but keeps his eyes averted. All he can see are his father's mottled hands, like meat that has spoiled in the sun. He remembers when those hands were tender and kind, when they threw him a ball. He remembers lots of things that serve no purpose now.

His father steps aside, and braces a rotten meat hand on Charlie's shoulder, assisting him to the uneven stairs. Rain trickles down the wall through the stains.

Charlie grabs the splintered railing and eases himself down one step at a time, the threadbare carpet squelching beneath his feet. He is exhausted by the time he reaches the bottom where mildew has turned the floor black. Fungi have sprouted like cartoon umbrellas in the corners as he leans against the door, presses his brow to the spongy wood to catch his breath.

"Go on," urges his father. "She won't wait for you forever and you may never be able to go outside again. Go."

He pushes away from the door, looks at the depression in the wood where he pressed too hard against it, and reaches for the handle. As his fingers find the rusted metal, he suddenly becomes aware that the pockmarked wood, through which the grey light of day seeps through, reveals only darkness now.

Someone is outside, waiting.

She is waiting.

With a smile it hurts him to maintain, he yanks the door wide.

His heart halts its beating, his mind bursts into flame.

"Come," says the girl with the violet eyes, and holds out her hand. Warmth of a kind he can't recall experiencing before floods through him, and his pain ebbs away. He thinks she might be an angel, the miracle every man and woman who still has their tongue spends their days demanding from whatever exists beyond the turbulent sky. He considers asking her, but as soon as they're clear of the cul-de-sac and into the grass leading to the ruins of the parking garage, she lets him go. He expects to fall, to be embarrassed by his frailty before the one person left to impress, but his legs hold. Not only that, but he finds he can put all his weight on them, one at a time, and they do not buckle. "Thank you," he says, but she has moved ahead of him and he can't be sure she has heard. While he is debating whether he should repeat himself, she replies.

"I did nothing. Thank *her*."

He does not speak again until they are in the shadow of the enormous garage, six stories high and so overgrown it appears to be made from the trees. With endless rain, the woods have grown bold. The concrete façade has been suffocated beneath cauls of ivy. Verdant veins thread their way to the roof. The door is not a natural one, but a puncture wound, as evidenced by the ragged edges and trailing cracks around the trunk of the ash tree that has forced its way out into the grey light. Garlands of ivy and moss provide a screen against the rain and it is beneath this the girl ducks, and then she is gone. Charlie wants to ask her to wait for him, because now, for the first time, his excitement is eclipsed by unease. What if this is a lure, a trick? What if she is in league with The Cruel Boys and they're waiting inside to smash his bones with their steel rods and wooden bats?

It is now, he realizes, too late for such terrors. He has already been out in the drizzle long enough for mold to have sprouted around his collar and sleeves. There is every chance that his parents will refuse to let him back inside, though there is little risk of making them sick when they are already dying. But he is aware that he has given them all the excuse they need to be rid of him if that is what they desire. Rather than give them that chance, he swallows his fear and follows the girl through the aperture into the garage.

Inside are candles and warmth and little mold. It is possible that the vegetation has protected this enormous room from the worst of the moisture, though that seems unlikely. He doesn't dwell on it, however. His attention is drawn to the large circle of candles around the wide pillar in the center of the room and the figure they illuminate.

Hypnotized, grateful for the heat, he moves close enough to see that a woman has been lashed to the pillar using ropes made from braided ivy. They encircle her wrists, her throat and her feet. Her face is obscured by a mask fashioned from the skull of an animal he cannot identify. A cow, perhaps. He wouldn't know. He has never seen one, only heard of them from his father.

Several large notebooks have been scattered around the woman's feet. The covers alternate between dark red and vibrant yellow. Each one bears a different title, written in thick black letters. Charlie edges close enough to read the nearest of them: THE HOUSE ON ABIGAIL LANE, A WICKED THIRST, TRAVELER.

"You must read them," says the girl, startling him. She is standing behind him. He can smell her breath and it offends his nose. She smells very much like his father.

"Why?" he asks, despite feeling as though he shouldn't.

The girl's eyes are luminous in the candlelight. Her teeth are too thin, the gaps between them too large, but her skin is pristine like marble. "So you can be free," she tells him. "And so you can be blessed by The Bone Mother." Her voice sounds like the rain. He looks from the notebooks to the effigy tied to the pillar.

"Can she fix me?"

"There is nothing to fix."

"And the pain?"

"Education. Don't you wish to learn?"

He frowns. "I wish to be away from here, but wishes don't come true."

"The Bone Mother disagrees."

At that, the effigy moves and he jerks back a step, aware for the first time of the glint in the eyeholes of the mask. She is awake, and aware, and watching, and he feels the force of her expectation.

"Read the stories, Charlie. Open your eyes to the truth."

He is no longer sure he wants to be here with the strange girl and the thing tied to the pillar, but he knows there is nowhere to go. If he tried to run, the ability to do so could be stripped from him as easily as it was given and there is only so much shame he can take.

He moves to the candles and, forgetting that it is no longer necessary to employ such caution, slowly lowers himself down onto the concrete floor. He reaches for the nearest story: THE LAND OF SUNSHINE.

"Read, Charlie," he is told, by more voices than one.

So he does.

THE LAND OF SUNSHINE

THE CRACKS IN HIS MARRIAGE had started to appear ever since the affair, and nothing they had tried in the years since had fully shored up the crevasse. It didn't help that his wife couldn't speak, for though it had never bothered him before, her muteness now more than ever seemed like an infirmity destined to compound the inevitability of their dissolution. He had never heard her voice, and so did not have the right to mourn its absence. She had ceased speaking due to a trauma that long preceded their union. But still, it frustrated him. She could hear him perfectly, of course. This, he knew. But without the benefit of inflection, her silent nods or shakes of head, or the slight gestures she made with her hands could only be read one way, or no way at all, and he needed the kind of closure the quiet seldom gave. She had never learned to sign, and he supposed this was a good thing. If her hands were not raised, he didn't have to see the pale scars that bisected her wrists, and thus be reminded of how he had failed her.

To aggravate the situation, as they moved like ghosts through the gloaming of their lives together, he also began to develop the nagging sensation that something other than love had gone missing, something other than his loyalty had gone astray. It manifested itself as a vague certainty, a low voice in another room, the persistent conviction that someone had stolen into the house of their marriage and shifted things around just the tiniest little bit, just enough to create a subliminal feeling of violation, of something not quite amiss, but awry.

When he expressed this concern, his wife regarded him as she often did these days, with mute attentiveness draped like a dust cloth over the dark hunkering shapes of pity and resentment. If she felt the same absence of anything but mutual love, it was not evident on her face, but then nothing was.

It was at night, as he lay on his back in a bed that like so many things had seen better days, his back sunken into the valley in the old mattress, that it became clear what he must do. He must find and locate that missing thing, that wrong thing, and return it from whence it came, before he lost all that was left to lose.

After creeping wraith-like out of their bedroom, which seemed cavernous in the dark—a direct contrast to the lives shrinking within its suspiciously wavering confines—he decided to start at Moriarty's, a place he had frequented enough times that surely the mahogany on his favored corner of the bar must still bear the scuffs of his elbows.

Dressed in a once-black threadbare overcoat and pork pie hat, he shuddered out into the cold and navigated the narrow dark streets with the same chaotic certainty as a marble through a tilted maze. Here in this forgotten neighborhood, the streetlights had died in time with the idea of prosperity and reclamation. The city had eaten it, and its coal-dark shadow had scalded everything from the gaps in the gutters to the morality of the disillusioned young who haunted its corners. Even they weren't present now though, and his sigh of relief was visible as a transient specter that, despite the absence of a breeze to claim it, whipped away from him as if eager to be free of the association. In the suffocating quiet, his shoes made the sound of slow sarcastic applause in the dry, humorless rent of an alley which seemed all too eager to close in on him before he had a chance to clear it.

Freed of the garbage-truck like sensation of being crushed as flotsam, an impression aided by the stench that swaddled him upon his exit, he moved quickly toward the sole oasis of light in this otherwise claustrophobic urban labyrinth of forgotten streets and found himself within view of the bar. It sat crookedly on a corner that seemed merely to tolerate the weight, the amber light through the stained windows bleeding sickly into the gloom.

Buoyed at the reprieve from the darkness, the man quickened his step and then immediately regretted it, his enthusiasm writing signatures across his knees with an arthritic pen. Hissing like the steam that bullied its way from the vents in the street, he limped on, until he found his heart lightened by the idea of old friends and familiar faces, his hand warmed by the door handle, his mind settled, but only briefly, by the notion that here the mystery of loss might begin its unravelling.

He twisted the handle and pulled.

The door was locked, the single ratcheting cough it gave as abrasive as the poorly concealed laughter of pranksters.

He tried to peer through the frosted glass and made out only a series of still shapes clustered in a tableau around a bar, their blurred shadows paler toward the top where their faces were turned toward the door. The thought of knocking raised his fist. Uncertainty kept it an inch from the glass. Clearly, they knew he was here, and just as clearly, he knew he was not wanted within. But did they know who was standing upon their threshold? The weight of his own guilt this night told him they probably did, and that they had latched the door as soon as they heard the unsteady echo of his approach.

Still he stood, as still as they, and for a moment not even air nor light seemed to move, his shadow flung across the curb behind him as if the decision to depart had already been made. Moments passed, a part of him daring, wishing someone to let their own guilt sway their opinion by carrying them to the door to admit him, but no one moved, still they stared, and at last he placed a palm flat against the cold glass as if wishing it farewell, and moved away.

The memory of their faces split by smiles assailed him as he followed the cracks in the pavement with his eyes, but the more he remembered, the uglier those smiles became, the once bright eyes above them darkening like ink spilled in water, accusation and judgment flashing like silvery fish in the ocular depths. He shook his head to clear it and raised his eyes through the sudden veil of rain he was almost arrogant enough to believe had been sent solely to torment him. It hissed malignantly down around him, filling the holes in the pavement, seeping up through the battered leather soles of his shoes, and running in rivulets down the fissures in his face. With the rain came a cold that insinuated its way through the coat and his skin and settled in his bones. His body stiffened, the pain in his knees worsening until he was forced to stop and lean against a red brick wall emblazoned with graffiti that had long ago lost its vibrant rebellious color to the smoke and dust and decay that formed the breath of this dying place.

It would be so easy to give up, he knew, as he let his brow rest against the back of his hand, the rain tapping against the brim of his hat. It would be the easiest thing in the world to tamp down the compulsion that had plagued him of late. It was merely unfinished business, after all, and what life is not characterized by such things? Not everything gets to end. Sometimes you walk out of the theater before the movie is done, and never give it a second thought. How simple it would be to do the same now. Besides, despite the need within him to find whatever it was he had lost, perhaps it was his destiny to exist in a house haunted by the ghost of old love. What man didn't suffer that melancholic torment at one time or another? He could use the pain as an excuse, for now it felt as if someone had struck his knees with a crowbar. Imaginary points of contact radiated fire. Hissing air through his teeth, he straightened, looked back the way he came, then ahead to where the ruined pathway. All was darkness there, the streetlights long broken and bent almost double so that they formed a steel ribcage around the street.

He could go home, but the thought of the silence awaiting him there kept him for the moment immobile, stricken by the kind of uncertainty that forces men to merely occupy their lives instead of living them. At the root of it all was a gnawing absence, a dark hollow within him from which something had been removed, something so critical to his composition he had grown to fear he might die if he didn't recover it.

He moved back from the smoke-stained wall and raised his face to the sky. Towering above him was a billboard he had to blink the rain away to fully appreciate. The same dilapidation that had scoured the town of definition had not been dissuaded by the height at which the billboard stood. On its scabrous surface he saw a once gleaming silver airplane which had been shorn in half by the peeling of the paper upon which it had been printed. Beneath the aircraft, the tropical ocean looked speckled with ash and flotsam. To the right of the bisected plane, a man and woman clinked glasses full of mildew, their faces torn away by decay and hanging in yellowed flaps from their necks. Above it all was the message THE LAND OF SUNSHINE in large yellow block capitals, and though most of the letters were missing from the cursive text beneath, he was, after sleeving the rain from his eyes, able to put it together: WHAT ARE *YOU* WAITING FOR?

It seemed ominously appropriate, and as he lowered his face and spat rain, his breath like the chug of a steam engine, he decided to keep moving forward. Behind him was a life that had been robbed of love and color. Ahead might be the possibility of salvation, or at the very least, a kind of closure. If that closure came in the form of his own expiration on the sodden streets of this caliginous city, then so be it. It would still be an end, and that, he knew, was what was needed, was all that was even remotely attainable at this late hour.

But as he walked, something else began to nag at him. Head bowed against the strengthening deluge, he thought again of the sign. It had once been an advertisement for a travel agency, a summons to the sedentary to leave it all behind in favor of an escape, of a temporary reprieve from the familiar and the mundane. Respite from the gloom so pervasive here. Given the proximity of the billboard to his house, he was not surprised that he remembered it, but there was something else about the sign or the message it conveyed that thrummed a chord deep in his chest and brain, something that suggested he did in fact, at some point in his sixty years, accept that invitation. But if that was true, he recalled nothing about the destination, retained no warm memory of sunshine or tropical beaches. There was only the vague notion that he had once upon a time not been where he was now, the billboard triggering the synaptic suggestion that THE LAND OF SUNSHINE had been where he'd ended up. If so, he wished he could remember, for even the notion of such a place perforated a pinhole of light in the wall of black behind his eyes.

The street curved to the left, the cracked macadam giving way to cobblestone that glistened like gray boils in the rain. Here the street grew narrow again, the tops of the buildings leaning over on both sides as if eager to engage in congress with their brethren. As he squinted into the murky light, the source of which eluded him, he saw a shadow detach itself from a doorway on the left, cross the street, and scurry into another on the right. Another few steps, his knees aflame, and he discerned that it was from this building the foggy feeble light emerged.

For a long time, he watched that building, the memory of it the tip of an iceberg in frigid water, the greater truth an immense form beneath the surface. He was cold, so cold now, his muscles aching from the strain of not relenting to the shivers that danced in his bones. He would have to enter that building if only for the shelter, but even as this awareness settled upon him, he knew it was a deception. There was another, much more significant and infinitely awful reason why that building was here, why he was here, dallying on the threshold. This was where the night had been leading him all along. It was why his old and long-lost friends at the bar had not admitted him. To do so would have been to halt the greater journey, to deny him his ultimate destination, to muddy his thoughts with saccharine sentimentality when the time and opportunity to indulge in such things was long gone.

He was here, without fully knowing where here was, unable to move as surely as if his feet had grown roots to bind him to the rain-slick cobblestones.

Again, the sign: THE LAND OF SUNSHINE.

And: WHAT ARE *YOU* WAITING FOR?

He knew what he was waiting for. Here, in oblivion, there was no further hurt, no revelation that might destroy him, reduce him to a further degree of nothing. Here, right now, he was still safe in ignorance, even as he admitted to himself that that had never really been the case. Not really. There had been inklings and suspicions, decades spent close to home for fear of seeing the cues Out There that would force him to accept what had been done, force him to come face to face with whatever entity had expelled him from The Land of Sunshine and erased even the tiniest recollection of the happiness he had found there.

Here, in that building, the answer, the closure he sought, awaited.

And so, frozen on this cold wet street, he would not move.

On the first floor of the building into which the man had run, dirty yellow light began to breathe through a mullioned window.

He watched that jaundiced light, watched it swim as figures moved within it, and in an instant, knew who was there.

In agony, he forced himself to move, his legs feeling as if metal spikes had been driven through the soles of his feet into his thighs and found himself in the doorway. It was open, revealing an old wooden stairway littered with trash. The walls were marred with smudged handprints, perverse messages, and crude cartoons written with whatever the author had had on hand. He ignored them as he grabbed with a shaky hand the equally unsteady balustrade and hoisted himself up the steps. On the landing above, a light hung from a fraying cord, the bulb stained and smoking, filling the stairwell with the smell of burning dust.

There was no sound from up there, only his breathless grunting and the shuffle and squelch of his saturated shoes on the steps.

Halfway up the stairs, a figure appeared on the landing, and stood for a moment looking down at him. It was a man, his angular face lined and haunted, his eyes like pools of oil, the sockets turned to shadowed craters by his position beneath the naked light. He held his hands together like a man about to pray.

"You too?" he said.

The old man did not reply, but, possessed of the absolute certainty that an affirmative response was in every way the correct one, nodded slightly.

The man's passage down the stairs felt like a hollow breeze, his feet making not a sound on the steps, and then he was gone.

The old man took a breath and continued upward until his face was level with the landing and he could see the stranger's footprints in the thick layer of dust on the floorboards. With gnarled, aching fingers, he reached the landing almost on all fours, and collapsed against the wall, his trembling body obscuring the salacious script tattooed upon the crumbling green paint.

Behind his eyes, veils were falling away. He did not want to be here, shouldn't have come, but this was, for his purposes, exactly where he needed to be. He thought of his wife sitting quietly at home, not blind but refusing to see him, refusing to hear him. Waiting. And now, finally, he knew what it was *she* was waiting for too.

To his right, a door stood slightly ajar, the light within flickering and casting strange shapes against the visible sliver of wall. A vintage song he could not place played on an old radio and reached him through curtains of billowing static. He slid along the wall until he was at the door, reached shaking fingers toward the wood, and gently prodded it further open. The hinges were mute; the door opened liquidly. He looked down at the threshold, at the long deep scratches in the wood, and knew if he was to change his mind about how this night would end, he would have to do it now.

Then, in an instant, the choice, assuming it had ever really been his, was removed. There came a shuffling scraping sound. Down on the floor, just inside the door, an ornate mahogany box was shoved into view. Behind it, a pale slim hand with chipped red fingernails withdrew, leaving him paralyzed with terror. He knew the owner of that hand; he had always known her.

WHAT ARE YOU WAITING FOR?

With great difficulty, he reached down and retrieved the box, fearful that the woman's hand would shoot out and latch onto his wrist. But she did not interfere, and there was no need. They were beyond that now.

He cradled the box, took a moment to wipe away the patina of dust with the heel of his hand, and moved his fingers to the latch. He unclasped it, then paused, suddenly possessed of a soul-shredding horror that almost took the legs out from under him. He staggered, the wall to his right the only thing that prevented his fall. Paint chips sprinkled to the floor. He could not breathe, could not keep his grip on the box, but was terrified to let it fall. Instead, he allowed himself to slide down the wall until he was sitting with his back to it and set the box down beside him. He closed his eyes only briefly, long enough to see dark red notes pulsing in the darkness there, and when he opened them again, she was standing before him, as he knew she would be.

This was the ending.

Amusement had characterized her strange face the night he had met her, and it was no different now. He did not recall, however, her skin being translucent enough to see the blue worms of her veins through it, or her eyes being quite so dark, her hair so dead, but then the years here had cloaked his mind in verdigris, and clearly if anything was absent from this place, it was the notion of beauty.

She said nothing, just stared down at him. Like her skin, the gown she wore was sheer enough to allow him to see what there was to see beneath it, but he had no desire to look. It was hard enough to look upon her face, with its queer smile and eyes that swam with malevolent cheer.

Once upon a time he had sought this woman out, willfully departed The Land of Sunshine to be with her, and with a few ropes and a carving knife, she had condemned him to The Land of Darkness, where he existed still. The answers and the memories had come slowly, but he had found them now, and felt a small pulse of satisfaction that he had been right all along in knowing something had been taken from him, and that she had been willing to give it back.

An eternity passed beneath her silent attention, until abruptly, and with a wider smile than he had seen thus far, one that tore the corners of her mouth and almost split her face in half, she leaned over and shoved her face into his, the sparks in her eyes burning coals in a dying fire, and she spoke two words on a breath of ashes.

"Go, lover."

Only when she was gone, the shadows on the wall revealing her orgiastic gyrations somewhere inside that room, the taste of ash on his tongue, did he get to his feet. The pain in his knees and hands was not nearly as bad as before. It had migrated to his chest and head. Like a drunken man, he staggered down the stairs, the memory of her burning eyes scalding his mind.

A short forever and he was outside on the street again, and alone. He was gratified at least to see that the rain had stopped.

His shadow vanished as the light behind him went out.

Without a look back at the building in which he had lost everything that mattered, he went home.

* * *

She was not awake when he entered the bedroom, and for this he was relieved. There was no reason to think that she would feel compelled to speak to him ever again or accept the words he offered as truth. But now there was an element of hope, the possibility of maybe. Resolution was a myth. Such a thing could never exist here. The best he could expect was some small degree of understanding, but maybe even that was preposterous.

Exhausted, he slipped out of his wet shoes and carefully lowered himself down onto the bed, where he sat for some indeterminate amount of time, long enough to see the sun not rise and the sky not lighten from anything other than permanent dark.

On his lap was the box, the clasp undone.

He thought again of the sign and remembered. Remembered the other place, where the sun indeed rose and the sky knew color other than black, which was no color at all, only the absence of it, and he remembered the warmth of that sun on his face, the light in his wife's eyes. He remembered knowing her love and filling her with his. There had been no shadows there, and he felt an ache at the loss of it because it was the only thing he could never get back.

Behind him, his wife stirred. He turned to look at her and saw that between the unkempt locks of her iron-gray hair, one blue eye regarded him coldly.

"I'm sorry," he said, and handed her the box.

She accepted it, but did not open it.

He removed his shirt and slipped into bed beside her, his hands by his sides, his eyes on the cracks in the ceiling he had grown to fear would one day open up and swallow him.

At some point in the night, his wife's fingers found the edges of the gaping cavity in his chest, but she did not replace what had in some other place and time been removed. Instead, she held the box close to her chest as if it were a child, and to him, that was just fine.

His heart belonged to her now, after all.

As he sank into sleep, he allowed himself the thought of a smile but did not allow it to reach his mouth. Even if he'd wanted to, he could not remember how.

No hope, perhaps, and no light, but some indefinable something in place of nothing.

For now, and forever, that would have to do.

TRAVELER

THIS IS THE STORY AS MY CAPTOR RELATED IT TO ME: Three weeks ago, on a rainy Monday morning, he, Ronald, was at work. His daughter, Sophie, was at school. His wife, Denise was here, at home, prepping a beef stew (Ronald's favorite.) There came a knock on the door. Though visitors were not uncommon—because, much to Ronald's chagrin, no matter how isolated your house is, people will always find you—Denise was probably surprised. It was not yet noon, and guests at *that* hour was unusual. She went to the door. Upon opening it, she found me standing there. After that, one must resort to theory and speculation. What *is* known is that whatever transpired between the moment she admitted me, and the time Ronald arrived home, it left Denise dead in the bath tub. The prevailing theory was that I was the responsible party, and, considering the evidence, any court in the country would have condemned me just as poor Ronald did.

All he had to go on were the basic facts:

When he left, she was alive. When he returned, she wasn't, and I was sitting naked on his sofa covered in her blood, a hacksaw in my hands. What would *you* think? It was, what the judicial system would have considered an open-and-shut case. But Ronald was not going to give them the opportunity to waste good taxpayer money on me with a trial. No. He was going to handle that himself and again, who could blame him? You might, in your grief and rage, feel compelled to do the same. Why take the risk of something going wrong, of a lawyer fucking it up, or some government employee mislabeling evidence? Granted, such things don't happen often, but to Ronald, who came home to find his wife missing her head, hands, and feet, it was a time for aberrations and thus, the ordinary rules of the universe no longer applied.

I didn't resist, let him beat me unconscious, and when I woke, I was tied to a chair in the basement. He was sitting across from me, his face a horrible thing to behold. He was pale, sweaty, his eyes huge and filled with pain, his mouth hanging open slightly. He was holding the hacksaw with obvious intent.

"Who are you?" he asked.

"Mike Hannigan. Who are you?"

"Ronald Jenkins. Why did you do this? Why did you come into my home and...and do what you did to my wife? How could you hurt my wife?"

"I don't know."

"You don't *know?*"

"No. I don't remember doing anything. I don't even know where I am."

He lunged at me then and dragged the teeth of the saw across the meat of my right thigh. I screamed in pain, and he looked visibly surprised at my reaction, as if, given what I'd done, he assumed me incapable of any kind of feeling at all. He jerked back and looked down at the wound, which, though not life-threatening, was wide enough for the blood to pool and trickle down the sides of my leg. I clenched my teeth against the pain from both the wound and the rope biting into my wrists.

"I'm not going to accept 'I don't know.' You're going to explain to me why you did this, and then I'm going to do to you what you did to my wife. And I'm going to do it slowly, do you understand?"

"No, I don't understand. I wasn't here, and then I was, and now you're telling me I did something terrible and I don't know what it was or how it happened."

He spent the next ten minutes detailing what I'd done. I threw up twice. Then he rose from his chair and stood before me, that bloodied hacksaw held in a white-knuckle grip. He looked as insane as I'm sure he thought me, and I wondered if this was the moment in which I'd die. There was no calm acceptance on my part. I felt as if I'd awoken into some bizarre dream, some suffocating nightmare, and with each second that passed, I struggled against the reality of it. Ronald had no reason to believe me, so he didn't. He was a six-foot-tall maelstrom of emotion and he channeled all of it into a broadside swing of the hacksaw that took most of the right side of my face with it as neatly as someone snatching a doily off a mahogany table.

The pain was epic and unprecedented, and I was blessed with the briefest moment of unconsciousness before he slapped me violently awake where the agony was waiting. His face filled my world, his eyes maddened by grief.

"Tell me why you did it."

"I can't remember. I swear I can't."

He hit me again. My head lolled back. I tasted my own blood.

"Do you not understand that I'm going to murder you? That I'm going to cut you to pieces? Why did you kill my wife? Why? Why? Why?"

Each time he repeated the question he punched me in the face. Again, the pain spirited me away, and again, he roused me with a sharp blow to the face. This time when the room swung unsteadily back into view, all I saw were metal teeth. He had the hacksaw braced a mere inch from my eyes. And he was weeping.

"I will cut them out, you fuck. I will cut out your fucking eyes, I swear."

"I'm an accountant."

"What? What did you say?"

"I'm an accountant. I work at Hyam & Grace, a firm in Brooklyn. Call them. They'll tell you. Or...or Google it. That's where I work. I was there yesterday, or at least, what I think was yesterday. A man came into the office. Some weird guy. He...there was something badly wrong with him. With his eyes. Cold. Weird colors. I remember feeling...I remember being frightened. He just stood in my office looking up at the ceiling. And his clothes—"

"Why the fuck are you telling me this? I want you to explain to me why you—"

"His clothes...moved. Something about the patterns. There were marks too, designs on his neck and hands."

He punched me square in the face and the force of the blow snapped my head back. The chair tipped over backward, and my shoulder blades knifed the concrete floor, knocking the wind from my lungs. My vision swam. I saw stars that reminded me too much of that customer's eyes, and then Ronald was looming over me. I felt pressure on my throat, couldn't breathe.

"I'm going to give you some time to think, not because I'm possessed of any sense of mercy or pity, but because my daughter's coming home soon to the worst day of her life. When I come back, you're going to tell me why you killed my...why you killed my *wife*. And once you do, I'm going to start taking you apart, piece by piece."

He pressed his boot down on my throat until the world went black.

* * *

I dreamed strange dreams, of black figures swimming in a deep red sea, of cobalt suns and mammoth creatures shrieking at the stars, and then I was rising back into consciousness. An hour, a day, or a month might have passed. I saw through swollen eyes a pale young girl kneeling before me. She was weeping silently, tending to my injured face with visible sorrow and confusion and hate. I felt myself reaching out to her, the desire to speak, to tell her I was sorry, to touch her, but my body was frozen, my lips stuck together with dried blood, and I could only moan. She jolted as if struck and stared at me, eyes wide. Then she was gone, her footsteps distant echoes on the stairs. Then the door slammed shut, a latch slid home, and I was once more submerged.

"Wake the fuck up."

The shock of the cold water was enough to summon a scream, but the renewed agony closed my throat. I hurt all over, except for the numbness in my arms. My hands may as well have been dead crabs glued to my wrists. My knee burned; the right side of my face raged as if hot coals had been embedded beneath the skin. One eye was swollen shut, and my mouth felt stuffed with cotton. I raised my head as much as I was able. Ronald had set me upright again and stood a few feet away. Gone was the hacksaw. Now he had a hammer and a box of nails and the sight of them, set so casually next to his chair, filled me with atavistic dread. He set the bucket down.

With great and painful effort, I forced my lips apart, heard the crack of the bloody crust.

"Please..."

"Are you ready to talk now?"

I could only nod, aware that if I didn't at least try to appease him, I was going to die. I realized my death was an imminent reality, but there was no reason I should hasten it, at least not until the pain grew to be too much.

"I'm sorry for what I did to your wife. Please believe me when I tell you I have no memory of doing it. I have no memory of traveling three hundred miles from my office to your house and hurting anyone. It wasn't...it isn't me. I'm just a normal guy. I have a job I hate, a wife I love, a dog who shits everywhere whenever he hears a sound louder than a squeak. I drink a little too much. I haven't spoken to my parents in ten years. I have a scar and arthritis in my right hand from when I caught it in a machine press back in my teens. I voted Republican for no better reason than I knew it'd piss off my father."

Seated across from me, Ronald stared with open hostility, but there was something else there too, something I had hoped and prayed to see and thought impossible. It was the tiniest vestige of uncertainty.

"There's no car outside," he said. "I walked a mile up the road in both directions. Nearest bus stop is thirty miles away. How did you get here?"

"I have no fucking clue. I don't even recall leaving my office."

"Why us? Why my family?"

"I don't know."

"Then what *do* you know, because if your mind's a blank, you're no use to me and we might as well just get to the business of ending you right now."

"Like I said, I was at work. That guy I mentioned. He just...I didn't even see him come in. He was just there, standing in front of me. Real fucking peculiar sort. Like seeing a homeless person in an expensive suit. Nothing about him fit. I remember...I remember asking him what his business was, and he smiled at me. Worst thing I've ever seen. I was instantly nauseous, as if when he'd opened *his* mouth, he'd breathed something foul into mine. 'I'm a traveler' he said, as if that explained anything, and he moved toward me. I got up, afraid he was going to attack me or something, and then..."

"And then?"

"And then I was sitting on your couch upstairs and it was you who was attacking me."

"Bullshit."

"I don't know how, but he did something to me."

"You're a fucking nut and I'm done listening to this."

"No, look, please, just listen. I'm telling you the truth. I know it won't change anything. I know your wife is dead and please believe me I am so fucking sorry for that, and I'm not telling you any of this so you'll let me go, or to torture you by not giving you what you need to hear...I'm telling you this because it's *all I know*. If you want to call the police on me, I'll go to jail and if I really did what you say I did, then I'll pay for my crimes. It's not like anyone's going to believe me. It's not like I even expect *you* to believe me. Just please, I beg you, please don't hurt me anymore."

He scooped up the hammer and rose. That doubt in his eyes was fading, replaced by the anger that had possessed him since he found me in his house and saw what I did to his wife. And I know I did it. I know I killed her. It's preposterous to think that I didn't. It's preposterous to think that I did. But all the evidence was there. I was found hundreds of miles from home covered in blood holding a hacksaw with a dead body in the tub. Doesn't take a fucking genius to connect the very obvious dots. But. I know without question that it wasn't really me. It couldn't have been. I could never do such a thing to anyone. I've never even been in a fight, for Chrissakes.

When I told Ronald this, he answered with the hammer.

* * *

For the next few days, I was left alone but for brief visits from Ronald's daughter. She tended to my wounds, shoved moldy bread into my mouth and washed it down with lukewarm water. I tried to speak to her, but she never lingered. As expected, she looked like a ghost. I shouldn't have tried to engage her. I know that now, knew it even then. I just needed her to know I was sorry, but she crammed that food into my mouth so violently, I couldn't, and she was always gone before I managed to swallow it.

* * *

I lose track of time.

* * *

Another day, another week, I was slapped awake and I looked up to see Ronald standing over me again. His face was a mask of rage, his eyes bulging, and all I could think was, *this is it. This is the moment of my death. Either that or he's going to hurt me so bad I'll pray for death, but I won't die. He'll let me heal and then start all over again until I truly lose my mind.*

"What did you say to her?" he asked.

I felt dread at my confusion. All this time he had been putting questions to me that I couldn't answer, and each time, it brought me ever closer to punishment, and to the end. But there was little I could do to appease him without knowing the answers he sought.

"I don't—"

"Don't fucking give me that. What did you say to Sophie?"

"Nothing. She doesn't let me speak. I tried to tell her I am sorry, but—"

He drew back his fist and I turned away, bracing myself for the pain.

When it didn't come, I looked back and saw that he had all but fallen into the chair opposite me. He was even paler than usual, his eyes ringed with dark bags. He looked sick, his breathing labored, raspy.

"I think I need to kill you," he told me, with no emotion at all.

My first instinct was to protest. The plea rushed up my sore throat on a desperate wave. But I caught it behind my teeth as something dawned on me. There I was, in more pain than I'd ever felt in my whole life. I spent most of my days here either passed out, weeping against the pain, or vomiting. My nose was broken, my face destroyed. The girl tried to treat my wounds, but she was not a doctor and it looked as if the wound on my leg was getting infected. I still couldn't open my right eye and that probably wasn't normal. I was hungry and thirsty and stinking of my own waste. However it happened, I was a murderer and a prisoner. If, stricken by some incomprehensible moment of charity—maybe the notion that he himself did not wish to become a murderer—Ronald turned me over to the police instead of killing me, what would happen then? I'd go to prison for the rest of my life, become a disgrace, a vile news story that would destroy my wife and parents' lives forever. And sure, I hated my parents for how they had treated me over the years, but not enough to cause them that kind of pain. What possible good, then, could come from the life for which I was trying to plead?

None at all.

So instead I told him, "I think you're right."

He raised his head only slightly and looked at me. "Would you tell me why you did this? As a favor to me? Will you give me that much so someday I'll have some hope of understanding all of this?"

"I want to. Really, I want to tell you what you need to hear, but if I did, I'd be making it up. I don't understand how any of this happened. I feel like I went to sleep and woke up on the moon. Something possessed me. That's all I can think of."

"We were married eighteen years, me and Denise. She was my best friend. Without her, I don't know how to go on, but I have to. I have to be there for Sophie. Whether or not I believe any of your craziness, and I'm inclined not to, it doesn't change the fact that you killed my best friend and left me to raise my daughter alone. And now you've broken my little girl too. So you see, if I don't punish you for it, how do I get to feel like I made a difference? How do I get to be her protector?"

I shrugged as much as I was able. "If it makes you feel any better, your behavior is the only thing I understand about any of this. If someone hurt my wife, I don't know that I wouldn't do the same thing you're doing. Vengeance matters. It's sometimes all we have left."

He looked strangely at me then, as if for the first time since he came home and stepped into our shared nightmare, he at last saw me as a human being. It was not what I'd intended, and not a ruse. I was, as I had been all along, only telling him the truth as I saw it. But with this truth, I had essentially just given him permission to kill me, and it rattled him.

He made an odd sound then as tears came in a sudden wave and I looked away as the sobs wracked his body. It was a terrible sound, the grief jolting him like bolts of electricity. From the corner of my eye I saw him fall out of the chair to his knees, saw him lower his face to the floor, grab fistfuls of his hair, and scream into the concrete.

"I'm sorry," I whispered. It had by then become a mantra, but I didn't know what else to say. "I'm so sorry."

He cried for what seemed like an eternity, and when he raised his face, the floor was damp beneath him. He stayed there on his knees looking up at me, occasionally wiping his nose on his sleeve. His eyes were red and raw, his face white as a blank page. Then he slowly reached behind him and picked up the hammer.

"I am too," he said, and shuffled closer to me. When he braced a hand on my knee to lever himself up, it split the wound and I winced in agony. Pus leaked from the encrusted edges. He withdrew with a grimace.

"I didn't mean to do that. I forgot."

I almost laughed. "I'm pretty sure I'll get over it."

He smiled grimly at the redundancy of his apology, and slowly got to his feet, his hand tightening around the handle of the hammer. Everything seemed very still in that moment, as if we were posing for a photograph entitled *"The Moment Before Death."* I closed my eyes and felt a hollow open in my chest at the thought of my wife, of Sarah, who was no doubt already missing me, wondering where I was. It broke my heart to think that she would never know what became of me. She'd report me missing in a few days and the police would find nothing. Doubtless, Ronald would bury me in a field somewhere and there I'd remain, my fate a mystery.

We had so much we wanted to do.

I chose not to ponder the why of it all for fear that I would go even more insane than I already assumed myself. One does not babble about mysterious visitors with blue-sun eyes and swirling coats as justification for murder and not reach the conclusion that there's something mentally amiss. Other than the tragedy I had caused this poor man and his daughter, this was as it should be. I was the lucky one. In a moment, I'd be free, leaving the nightmare behind for everyone else to live with.

"I wish I owned a gun," Ronald said. "I'd make it quicker. But I'll do the best I can."

I nodded my appreciation.

He started to raise the hammer.

At that moment, the door at the top of the stairs swung open with a shriek, and both me and Ronald flinched and looked in that direction.

"Dad?" Sophie called down.

Ronald swallowed, the hammer stalled halfway through its upward arc. "Don't come down here, honey. I'll be up in a few minutes."

"Something's wrong, Daddy. Please, you need to come look."

"Honey—"

"It's about Mom's body."

That froze us both. Ronald's jaw dropped open at the same time he let go of the hammer. It hit the floor, the claw-end chipping the concrete, and then he was gone, thundering up the stairs as if the house was on fire. I heard him ask Sophie "What do you mean?" and then the door slammed shut behind him.

Though I could not see them, I heard their progress on the floor above me, heard their voices but could not make out the words. I tried not to let hope bloom in my chest. Nothing short of a life-rewriting miracle was going to undo what had been done here. What *I* had done here. And yet I couldn't help it. Sophie's timing seemed rather convenient, like divine intervention, *deux ex machina* designed to keep me alive a little while longer, if not commute my sentence entirely. But when I tried to imagine what Sophie had meant by her words, my imagination failed me. *It's about Mom's body.* What could possibly have happened to it to justify her interruption of her father's business with me? She had to have guessed what he was doing. He might even have told her in an effort to salve the all-consuming grief of her mother's death. *Don't worry, honey. Tonight, I'll make him pay for what he did.*

I listened to the muffled noises overhead until I grew weary, and despite my anxiety, or perhaps because of it, I drifted off.

* * *

"Wake up."

It was a struggle against a tidal current to do as I'd been asked. I felt mired in mud, my body sluggish, my blood turned to tar. It was as if I had been asleep and bound for months. My body sang with pain.

At length, I found the strength to open my good eye.

Sophie stood before me. "Good," she said, and took a step back.

I blinked to force her into focus, and when at last she gained definition, I saw that she was soaked from head to toe in blood like the prom girl from that Stephen King movie.

"What's...?" My head turned on muscles that felt like rusted cables. "What's happening?" *They must have chopped up her body*, I thought, and then immediately dismissed that as madness. What kind of a man forces his daughter to help him dispose of her mother's body? But if not that, then where had all the blood come from?

"His throat, mostly," Sophie said, and I blinked a few more times to appraise her anew. "It never ceases to amaze me how much and how easily you people bleed." When she stared straight at me, I saw that her eyes were the brightest lights in the room. Bright enough to send shadows dancing across the walls. Cobalt stars moving and shifting around the black holes of her pupils.

"Who are you?" I asked her, suddenly more terrified of her than I had ever been of her father, now lying dead somewhere upstairs.

"I would think you'd know," she said. Something thin moved beneath the skin of her face and left ripples in its wake, as if she were made of milk. "After all, we traveled here together."

I shook my head in denial of what I was seeing, of everything that had happened.

"I came to you," she said, rising from her seat. "I used you to get me here. I slaughtered the woman, and once they bound you, I jumped into..." She grinned and indicated the sixteen-year-old girl's body. "...well, *me*."

It came to me then, the look of shock on Sophie's face when I'd tried to talk to her. No, not talk. When I'd tried to *reach* her. She'd jolted because something had jumped from me into her, infecting her, possessing her. The Traveler, switching rides.

"Why are you doing this to me?" I asked, hating the fear and self-pity in my voice. "I've done nothing to you."

The Traveler's face darkened. "Haven't you? Haven't you *all* done something to us?"

"Who? Who's us?"

"Your betters."

"I don't know what that means. Please, just let me go."

The girl laughed with the sound of gravel crunching underfoot. "You're already free to go. Your hands have been unbound for days." She folded her arms, her misaligned face crinkled in amusement.

Though it took me a while, I realized The Traveler had spoken the truth. My arms had been freed, but it had been so long since I'd used them, and they were so drained of blood, I couldn't move them. I stood and realized the same thing applied to my legs. I pitched forward but did not fall. The Traveler's hand on my throat arrested my descent and those eyes became my world, and when I dropped to my knees, she mirrored the movement. We knelt on the concrete floor together like penitents. The room around us began to shimmer. Threads of ink unraveled in the air. I sensed rather than saw the impatient pacing of enormous things above and below where I sat in thrall. Felt a multitude of eyes regarding me with tangible hate.

My body began to quake as The Traveler brought her face closer to mine. Beneath her skin, the veins were moving, rearranging themselves into topographical maps of alien places. And above them, her eyes, ancient suns blazing, burning their way into my mind. I saw things of which I would never speak as my tongue turned to ash in my mouth and my lips began to burn. My flesh began to shrivel, to turn to stone, my teeth cracking, gums rupturing, eyes bleeding...

"Upon the altar," said The Traveler, "Your skin will dress The Prince."

I felt myself changing, being reduced to nothing, a dying star in a monstrous universe.

And then...

My hand. It twitched, the nails scratching the concrete. In my daze, I realized I was still here, still in the basement no matter the intrusive illusion of this alien thing and her abhorrent display. I moved my hand and The Traveler's eyes shifted in that direction. She spotted Ronald's hammer, and smiled as my fingers found it, dragged it, grabbed it and swung it toward eyes burning bright with amusement.

* * *

Wake up...

Before me stood a policeman, his hand still raised to knock on the door, but now his attention was no longer on that door or the man who stood holding it open before him. He was looking up toward his hat and the claw hammer that protruded from it, a quizzical expression on his face that only vanished when the blood began to flow. With a soft sigh, he collapsed against the wall, tumbled over onto his face and was still.

I looked up, confused, into the flashing lights of the police cruisers parked in Ronald's yard. A dozen or so police officers were screaming things at me, but I heard nothing but The Traveler's voice in my head, a maddening thing that made my skull vibrate with pain.

Stricken, I turned and looked back over my shoulder at the bodies of the man and his wife and daughter spread out across the living room floor in some bizarre kind of human jigsaw puzzle and began to weep. It made no sound.

"The Prince awaits his clothes," said The Traveler.

I turned back to the police, knowing there was no place left to run.

"Come, now, or we'll let him come to *you*."

And ran anyway.

Right into the swirling cobalt lights.

THE MANNEQUIN CHALLENGE

THEO SAT IN HIS CAR BROODING for close to twenty minutes before killing the engine. There was still time to leave, still time to concede to the voice inside his head that told him this was a bad idea. He didn't do parties, festive or otherwise. To him, it was all a bunch of small talk and big expense with no reward at all. Thus, the notion of standing in a room off the clock with a bunch of people he could barely stand to be around during work hours made the muscles in his shoulders tense up until he felt like he'd forgotten to remove the hangar when he'd put on his coat.

He looked out across the dark parking lot to the block of lights on the second floor of the building in which he had worked for the past eleven years. In honor of the season, orange blinds had been installed in place of the customary Venetians. They were shut, but through them he could see the silhouettes of people dancing, guffawing, or swilling drinks. Multicolored spots of light flashed against the windows, presumably from some kind of disco machine. Theo rolled down his window and heard the faint rhythmic thump of a bass, as if the building had developed a heartbeat in the three hours since he'd gone home. A pair of corn dollies flanked the entrance, arms spread in idiot welcome. Black vinyl silhouettes of witches, bats, and haunted houses had been stuck all over the glass double doors. Those were going to be a nightmare to remove, and Theo didn't intend to be the one to do it.

No, sir. Let whomever put them there be responsible for their removal.

Squat pumpkins grinned toothily at him from the steps to the front doors, the candles in their heads flickering in the slight autumnal breeze.

Theo pictured the faces of the people in the office, many of whom would be drunk by now, some of them obnoxiously so. He imagined trying to navigate a room full of gyrating hips and flailing limbs, hooded eyes and insincere cheer, spilled drinks and dropped finger food, and shook his head. Keying the ignition, he felt reassured by the hum of the engine, which represented one of his most critical tenets: forward momentum. *Always be moving forward to the next place, the next goal, the next objective.* No, he was not the partying type. It represented stalled motion with no legitimate benefit. He couldn't even remember the last time he'd gone out in the afternoon to anything more exciting than a movie at the dollar theater (he'd be damned if he was going to suffer the exorbitant costs imposed by the bigger chains), or to walk his Labrador, Freddy around the neighborhood. Thinking of his beloved pet, dear uncomplicated and quiet Freddy, made him yearn for the warmth and familiarity of home, and he started to put the car in gear. Started, then stopped, his hands on the wheel at ten and two, eyes on the empty cars around his own, foot poised above the gas pedal.

Nothing about this idea appealed to him.

Nothing at all.

And yet...

And yet sometimes he found himself wishing that it did, that he would awake one morning with renewed vigor and a more adventurous outlook on what had, without him knowing, become a very dull and predictable existence. Oh, he couldn't deny that there was a certain comfort and security in routine, in knowing ahead of time how his day was going to play out. *A place for everything and everything in its place*, as his dear departed mother used to say, and though she had meant it in regard to neatness, he'd nevertheless applied it to his life as a whole. Still though, he hadn't always been quite so rigid, or so joyless. He'd never found it easy to make friends or be around other people, had certainly never been popular, but he'd had acquaintances, people with whom he'd enjoy the occasional meal, or a drink, while discussing topics of mutual interest. He'd played golf before the arthritis in his knees had removed the luxury, had wandered around town browsing the antique and book stores, or just to get out and see what there was to be seen. He'd had a charming little nook in a nearby Irish pub from which he could enjoy random encounters with strangers or watch the patrons and imagine life stories for them, only to stop when he realized that the lives he imagined were invariably better than his own. This created an enmity for them they had done nothing to deserve and he never went back there again.

His life was cheerless now, devoid of randomness, and without it, without the unexpected, what was there to do but sit at home and wait for his time to run out? He would be sixty next year, and the liver spots were already annexing patches of territory across his body. A glance in the rearview mirror showed a sad-eyed man with a hangdog face and a mouth that had forgotten how to smile.

He sighed.

Freddy could wait a little while longer.

Freddy would understand.

Theo killed the engine and, bracing himself against the chill and the uncertainty of the evening, stepped out of the car.

* * *

As he stowed his hands in the pockets of his jacket and walked the short distance to the door, he wondered if it was nothing more than manners or a sense of obligation that had led the employees to invite him to their Halloween party. His desk had, after all, been the only one that had survived the decorating blitz. When offered some orange and black crepe paper, he had nodded politely and then stowed it in his drawer. He had sat out the pumpkin carving during lunch break, preferring instead to utilize that time as it had been intended: for eating. And, perhaps most significantly, he was the only one who had come to work today not dressed in a costume other than the one required of him: his customary charcoal suit, of which he owned four. He'd noticed his coworkers noticing and assumed their disapproval would mark the end of their attempts to include him in their pointless celebrating.

The invitation waiting on his desk at the close of day said otherwise. He had stowed it in his briefcase with nary a glance, only to give it a proper inspection at home where he could do so without anyone assuming it indicated interest, or a commitment to attend. The invitation was a cheap photocopy, typical Halloween fare, pumpkins and bats all over the place. In comic sans, the message read:

OFFICE PARTY 2NITE!
8.30 TIL WHENEVER
PRIZES 4 BEST COSTUME
STAY 4 TRIVIA QUIZ & MANNEQUIN CHALENGE!
FOOD & DRINKS CURTESY OF MANAGEMENT

He reached the front door and hurried inside. Before him was the corridor leading to the administration office. To the right, a wide stairwell led up to the accounts office on the second floor. Here Theo lingered, plagued with renewed uncertainty, until the front doors swung open with a squeal behind him. Startled, he turned around and found himself face to face with a witch in green makeup, much like the one from *The Wizard of Oz*, complete with fake nose and ugly moles on her chin, though Theo was pretty sure he didn't remember *that* witch showing off so much cleavage.

"Hey, Theo," the girl he now recognized as Sally Thurston said as she hurried past him and mounted the stairs. "You waiting for someone?"

"Hello," he said, his response drowned out by the staccato sound of her stiletto heels clapping against the tile steps as she vanished up into the darkness. "No, I..." He trailed off and stared up the stairs, unsure what to do. He glanced at his watch. There was still time to leave but the more that presented itself as the best course of action, the more annoyed at himself he became.

"Suck it up, Theo," he mumbled, and headed up the stairs.

If regrets proved to be the cost of his uncharacteristic abandon, he could entertain them tomorrow. For now, there was little to be lost from popping in to show his face and say hello. Perhaps the gesture would be appreciated and remove some of the negative stigma he had quickly (and to be honest, willingly) generated for himself among his coworkers. Maybe they would look at him anew. And even if the change wasn't anything so dramatic, maybe they'd include him in more of their ventures. He was free to decline at any point, obviously, but wouldn't it be pleasant just to be asked?

Slightly out of breath, he reached the second-floor landing and shrugged off his jacket to look more casual, though it was unlikely to count for much given that, without it, he still looked dressed for work. Still, he told himself, baby steps.

He headed down the hallway to the accounts department. Here, too, the door was festooned with Halloween stickers. In the middle was a giant pumpkin wearing shades with the legend

HAPPY HOLLA-WEEN! printed under its crooked maw. Another orange shade had been drawn down over the glass, making it impossible to see inside. Theo touched the door handle and a jolt of static traveled up his arm, rendering it unpleasantly numb. Mid-scowl, he looked at the handle as if expecting to see a novelty buzzer attached to it. There was nothing there, but now Theo cocked his head slightly, listening for the sound that should have been there, that he only now realized he hadn't heard since he'd stepped out of the car.

He thought he might hear laughter.

He thought he might hear voices.

What he heard instead, was nothing at all.

He waited. Did the absence of that pulsing heartbeat mean the party had died?

A dreadful thought occurred to him, warring with curiosity to send him back down the stairs, outside to the car, and home to the comfort of the predictable.

Sally told them I'm here.

He imagined her hurrying into the office after running into him downstairs and waving to get everyone's attention. "Guys, you won't *believe* who showed up."

Had that indeed been the scenario, he wanted to believe their reaction had been benevolent surprise, and yet that's not how his luck had ever run, and thus he imagined hushed laughter, the rolling of eyes, the low whispers as they agreed as one to lock the door and pretend the party had ended. Worse, having run into Sally, they'd know *he'd* know they were deliberately shutting him out. *We'll show that old crank what we think of him. Shut off the music and stay quiet everyone. He'll go away soon...*

Paralyzed by indecision, Theo stared at the glass and the grinning pumpkin sticker. He knew he should go, but wasn't that giving them what they wanted? After all, cruel people only thrived because their victims did nothing. Sally had seen him. They knew he was here. If he turned around and went home, they'd laugh about it for the rest of the night and he'd be the butt of their jokes every day from this moment on. *Remember the night of the Halloween Party, when we locked the door on Old Man Theo?* He had come here to be more sociable, to get out of himself for a spell, to make friends a part of his forward momentum. Instead he found himself, as he so often had, automatically excluded for daring to try.

And that angered him.

So, no, he was not going to go home. Instead he would draw on every ounce of assertiveness and stay right here until they admitted him. He would be a part of this night if only to spite them, and would relish the discomfort on their faces when they realized their plan to make a fool of him had failed.

Nodding to himself, he raised a hand to knock on the shaded glass, but then thought better of it. No matter what they might want him to think, he was not a guest. This was where he worked, and he had an equal right to be here. He lowered his hand, grabbed the door handle, and raised an eyebrow in surprise when it opened easily before him.

※ ※ ※

He'd expected to find the office empty, all his coworkers in hiding, pretending the party was over so that Theo would go home. But they were there, all of them.

They just weren't moving.

As the door eased shut, Theo hung his coat on the rack inside the door, just as he did every morning, and stood there taking in the scene before him.

His coworkers had placed orange filters over the spotlights in the acoustic tile, which had the desired effect of making the room look like the inside of a candlelit cave. The disco lights he had seen from the parking lot continued to spin in the corners, but with no music to accompany them, they seemed more like emergency lights.

Death stood by the photocopy machine, a drink raised to its bony mouth. Beside it, a mummy leaned in close, its head resting affectionately on his shoulder. They were frozen in place, as if waiting for their picture to be taken. Beyond them in the aisles between the desks, more revelers were gathered. Hips were thrust out, faces were upraised, arms were akimbo, bodies pressed together, a menagerie of ghouls frozen in seductive thrall to the memory of music. They'd been dancing, clearly, but had, like everyone else in the room, stopped at the announcement of Theo's arrival.

Sophie, the witch, sat with one heel on the edge of her desk, her chair tilted back, a full drink in her hand. Sugar made the rim of her glass glisten. Strands of honey colored hair threaded out from beneath her black wig. She, too, was unmoving.

At the far end of the room, Frankenstein's monster and his bride were caught in an embrace, their pale lips touching. Theo caught a glimpse of tongue and quickly looked away. Between the couple and the dancers, Raggedy Ann had stalled with a tray of food in her hand.

There were perhaps sixteen people in all, every one of them in costume, every one of them playing statues.

"Very funny," Theo said aloud, forcing some cheer into his voice, because in truth, he didn't find it funny at all. Perhaps in the light of day he might have better appreciated the performance or the prank, or whatever it was, but in the sickly orange gloom, he found the sight of his coworkers all frozen in place a little unnerving. Even the sound of his own voice in a room devoid of all other sound startled him. Which, he supposed, was the intent. It was, after all, a Halloween party.

Still standing just inside the door and very much conscious of the fact that even though everyone was pretending to be frozen they could still see and hear him, he surreptitiously produced from his pocket the invitation. A brief scan and he pocketed it again. *Stay 4 Trivia Quiz and Mannequin Chalenge.* So, that's what this was. Everyone here was playing at being a mannequin, but to what end? And how long should he expect it to continue? And had they pulled this same trick on every guest or was he the sole target of their silly prank?

Feeling even more self-conscious simply by virtue of his mobility, he moved further into the room and stood among the statues. He looked around, at turns impressed and disquieted by the intensity of their focus. "Very good," he said again, smiling and nodding to show his approval, hoping it would be acknowledged somehow by one of his colleagues. But no one moved. Beneath the heavy makeup, voluminous orange wig, and big red nose, he recognized Jeremy Lowell from administration. Ordinarily a rather humorless and curt fellow, Theo was surprised, not only to see him in costume at a party, but engaged in this odd performance with the others.

"You must have been bored," he said, and grinned to show he was joking.

The clown didn't respond, didn't move. Instead, he continued staring across the room at where Sally sat looking bored. His thick-fingered hands were joined together as if praying, or, more likely, hoping, perhaps that Sally might be open to spending some time with him. Not that Theo could blame him. She was arguably the most attractive worker here. Even Theo had caught himself staring, caught himself wishing he were younger whenever she passed his desk and the scent of her perfume infiltrated his day. But he knew better than to make a fool of himself.

He almost laughed out loud at that, felt the bitter grin spread across his face.

Yes, it surely wouldn't do to make a fool of yourself.

The smile faded and he walked on toward the main aisle between the cubicles where the cluster of coworkers had stopped mid-dance. Though the whole thing was off-putting, and he felt like the outsider not being a part of it, he nevertheless had to admit that he found the whole thing impressive. It couldn't be easy to hold those poses for so long. And they were being *so* still. It really did appear as if they'd been frozen. He saw not a stumble of foot nor twitch of lip, heard not a rasp of breath, nor scuff of heel. That many of them were probably drunk too only made it even more astonishing. He knew he wouldn't last more than a minute in a given pose. Not only was it a physical challenge, it also flew in the face of his motto, his need to always be moving forward.

The revelers around him formed a cage of monsters. One of the men, a werewolf he suspected might be the clerk, Lenny Hall, notorious ladies' man (though one whose charms had failed to win Sally over) had his arms in the air as if reaching for the lights. His shirt was open, exposing a muscular chest covered in a patina of wiry black hair. An Elvira lookalike Theo didn't recognize had her hands on his pecs, her lips spread in a broad grin, eyes hooded with lustful appreciation. Theo frowned and watched them closely, unblinking, until his eyes stung. They were not moving. At all. He had looked at Lenny's chest to try and detect the rise and fall of the man's breathing.

And found none.

Against his better judgment, for surely this would be the moment when they would explode back to life and scare the living hell out of him, he reached a hand out and placed it, palm down, on

Lenny's right breast. After a few moments, he moved his hand up and held his fingers before the man's lips.

No heartbeat.

No breath.

Puzzled, Theo looked around at the gathering, all frozen, all perfectly motionless. If it was a prank, it was a mighty convincing one, but how were they doing it? It was making less sense the longer it went on. For example, the dancer in the schoolgirl costume—Veronica Dawson—was leaning backward in faux revolt from the spastic gyrations of her boyfriend Dean Nolan. She had one knee raised, her arms thrust up in the air, so the angle at which she was leaning should not have been sustainable for more than a few seconds. And yet she was holding it with no indication of strain at all.

"Okay," Theo said, stepping away from the dancers. "You got me. Good job, everyone."

They ignored him.

"I have to admit, this is very, very impressive. I'd love to know how you all pulled it off."

After a few moments, he moved to the girl with the food tray.

"Hi, Betty. What's good?"

Raggedy Ann stared robotically at some point to the left of his face.

He helped himself to some Ritz crackers and cheese cubes from her tray. *Management will provide the food*, he thought. *Cheapskates.*

"I should have come as Raggedy Andy," he quipped and chuckled around a mouthful of cheese. "What a pair we'd have made." As he spoke, a sliver of cracker flew from his lips and lodged in the white of her left eye. Theo gaped, a horrified apology surging up his throat that stalled when he realized she hadn't blinked, hadn't reacted or registered the intrusion at all. And he couldn't help it, he laughed. Laughed so hard he wept, and when he noticed that Betsy's offended eye was weeping too, the only reaction he'd seen from any of them thus far, another wave of mirth hit him until he was doubled over and coughing a mixture of crackers and cheese out onto the floor.

At length, the gales of laughter subsided, and he rose, wiped his eyes, and took another cube of cheese from her tray. He popped it into his mouth, leaving only the cocktail stick in his hand, which he regarded thoughtfully. Then he looked at Betty, her eye streaming tears, and let his gaze rove down her face and neck until he was staring at the ample swell of her bosom beneath the gingham material of her dress.

"What if I were to touch you? Would you move then?" he asked, and his voice sounded strange to his own ears in a way he didn't like. Indeed, he felt strange. The hair was prickling all over his body. His pulse raced; he could feel it ticking away in his dry throat as if he'd swallowed a watch. His body was trembling, and he felt warm, much too warm, and yet giddy at the same time. It was alarming, this new sensation, but not unwelcome. A small grin crept across his lips and stayed there. *Let them play*, he thought. *I can play too.* And with that, he grabbed a cluster of cheese cubes and slid them free of the sticks upon which they had been impaled and returned to the makeshift dance floor in the center of the main aisle.

"What about you?" he asked Lenny Hall, who was still holding his arms aloft. "How long are you going to keep this up or is it your intent to be the last one standing?"

When Lenny didn't answer and just kept on dancing without moving, Theo swallowed, moved in close and pricked the man's belly with the cocktail stick. He almost expected the skin to resist, to be solid like concrete, but it behaved the way skin is supposed to and dimpled under the tip of the needle. Theo chuckled drily, looked up at Lenny's face for a reaction, and pricked him again, this time hard enough to leave a tiny dot of blood on the wound.

"How about now, Lenny? You in there? You going to answer me?"

Lenny's head was thrown back, eyes to the ceiling, chiseled jaw jutting defiantly forward. He was smiling. Consequently, Theo's grin faded.

"You're very popular in this office," he said. "And I honestly never understood why. Your looks? Sure, you're not ugly, but those looks are already starting to fade and you're only...what, thirty, thirty-one? Is it the coke, you think?" He pricked Lenny again, harder this time, right under his nipple, and still the man did not react. "Oh yes, I've walked in on you snorting that stuff in the bathroom. You fancy yourself a celebrity, I think. I think you believe you're better than everyone here. You're not though." He stabbed Lenny with the little needle again and again and again as he spoke, until the orange sky of Lenny's chest was dotted with tiny red suns. "You know what I heard Betty say about you once?" He let his hand move down until it was poised before the man's crotch. "I overheard her say she bets that with an ego so big, you probably have a tiny..." He jabbed the man in the groin three times in succession. "...prick."

And still Lenny did not blink.

Theo looked at him strangely. What kind of a prank required this level of dedication? The answer of course was: none. This was not a prank, not some fun activity designed to mess with his head. No. This was something entirely different, the nature of which eluded him for the moment. But the genesis hardly mattered now because he was overcome with power, a sensation he could never remember feeling before. If these people refused to acknowledge him now the same way they refused to see him during the day, he was in a unique position to make them pay for that. It was almost as if he'd been granted special powers, like a superhero, his cause vengeance for the injustices he had suffered his whole life at the hands of others. And while on some level, his most human level, this struck him as patently ridiculous and inherently dangerous, it did not prevent him from returning to Betsy and her tray of hors d'oeuvres, where he stripped all the sticks from the cheese cubes and inserted one into each of her eyes. It reminded him of prepping olives for martinis, except of course, olives didn't burst when you skewered them.

With a plastic grin frozen on his face, he moved from person to person, stripping them naked and jabbing playfully at their faces and bodies and ignoring the heightening sense of panicked urgency that built in tandem with each punctured eye.

You can stop. You can go home. You can end this. The prank is real and you're falling for it, but it's the worst kind of prank, the kind intended to expose the monster inside you...

At some point the music resumed, but he did not hear it, no more than he heard the counsel of that voice deep down inside him.

But as the hour grew late and midnight crept ever nearer, a great sadness descended upon him. Any vestigial joy he might have felt perforating the fleshy disguises of his coworkers ebbed away, leaving him feeling hollow and guilty. He did not know what had come over him and he dropped the bloodied cocktail sticks in disgust. Ultimately, these people were not to blame for how he perceived himself and hurting them was only a cowardly substitute for hurting himself. And that's what really needed to be done.

He felt a black horror in his soul he doubted he would ever be able to remove and, dispirited, he made his way to the coatrack by the door. "I'm sorry," he muttered, as he watched his blood and fluid-soaked hands retrieve from the hook the same boring jacket he wore each and every day "Truly, I am."

Theo turned and took in the room, the statues all in states of disrepair, all naked, all bleeding, and it no longer seemed so strange that they were ignoring him, or the lengths to which they had gone to teach him a lesson that needed hearing. Tonight, Halloween night, his forward momentum would bring him to one last stop: home, and a drawer full of knifes he would use to remove himself from this life.

Freddy would understand.

For once, everybody would.

With one final nod of apology, he turned and quietly exited the room.

As soon as the latch clicked home, Sally Thurston plucked a cocktail stick from her eye and smiled at the others. One by one, they smiled back.

After a moment reserved to ensure Theo was truly gone and not lingering in the hall, the party resumed.

GO WARILY AFTER DARK

THE BOMBS FELL JUST AFTER MIDNIGHT.

They tell you to prepare for such things. There are drills, kits, leaflets and posters, stern voices instructing you over the radio, but nothing can prepare the human mind for the sound of the world coming down. It is as if the devil has felled God. It is thunder from above and below. It is the very earth sundering. It is a single prolonged moment of chaos and destruction.

It is The End.

For months, since the retaliatory statements from their chancellor, we had lived in fear that this day would come, but as the days stretched on and the weeks went by, we did what people in fear will do and reached a sort of numb acceptance infused with a vein of hopeful doubt. If they were truly going to attack the city, then where were they? Wouldn't they have struck already? What were they waiting for? Such frail hopes, however, were easily thwarted. The city had become lightless, blacked out so as not to make a target of itself, which seemed a rather pointless exercise when the enemy already knew where to strike. People walked blindly through the streets, narrowly avoided the cars and buses with their extinguished headlights, and stumbled on in a daze, confused at this new dark world in which they found themselves marooned.

The soldiers came with their portable shelters, little more than caged tables, cheap and shoddy forms of protection for those of us who did not have yards in which to build proper ones. They gave us gas masks and told us how to use them. Wear them always, they told us, and for a while we did, until our faces grew too hot and too sore, and the smell of the rubber gave us headaches. Mostly we sat around the rabbit hutch table and enjoyed the silence with tension making us as rigid as the chairs. And at night, we dutifully pulled down the black curtains and turned out all but the weakest of lights. In the feeble glow, we huddled together like the refugees we feared we'd one day become at the behest of an enemy to whom we had done nothing, and we listened. When we spoke, it was merely a whisper, as if the threat might not be limited to the skies above, as if night's dark agents might be abroad, faces pressed to the windows, ears attuned to the slightest of sounds.

Sleep became a luxury few could afford. Often, there were sirens, howling up into the night like a stricken animal pleading for mercy. Instantly, we woke from restless slumber, muscles tightening, bodies subconsciously braced for impact, for death. The hair on the body rose; the heart began to race. The children, still sleepy headed, hurried into my arms, as if that could ever be adequate protection. My husband stood guard by the window, peeking through the tiny perforation in the black plastic. And always, there was nothing to report. By the time the sirens fell silent again, sleep had fled. Exhausted, we lay on the floor staring up at the cracks in the ceiling, thinking them nothing less than the blueprint of its destruction.

During the day, my husband worked. He was gone by dawn, drunk by six.

I sent the children to school where I knew they could learn nothing, washed their clothes, tried to keep up the pretense that this was still our home and not a brick prison waiting to collapse. It made my dutiful ministrations seem foolish. Bombs care little for scrubbed floors. To counter the malaise, I played scratched music on the tired Victrola, but found no reprieve in the rapturous heights of those arias. Instead, I was stricken by the profound and long delayed realization that, quite often, those women sung of war and tragedy, grief and loss. Thus, it was not joy I heard in their heavenly voices, but sorrow and anger. I felt no kinship with these strangers. Many of them had already died, the others away where windows did not need to be blackened and voices did not need to be muted. Safe.

For much of the day, I sat in silence and stared at the cracks above my head, the pattern that portended a terrible fate, and waited for my children to come home, my nose filled with the acrid stench of smoke from fires I couldn't see.

*   *   *

The night the bombs fell, the children were sleeping. We had moved them down into the basement, a closet sized room with a dirt floor and walls of hardened clay, the shoddy joists making it seem more like the gullet of some diseased animal than a sanctuary. It had been presented by the soldiers as a haven, a better bet, in any case, than the exposure of the main floor. Both my husband and I had resisted, and when we spoke of it amongst ourselves, the suggestion was instantly dismissed by the tone used to convey it as a possibility. Without knowing why, we did not want to send our children down there into the dirty dark. We had lived in the house for six years by then and had ventured into the basement only a handful of times, three of those without clear reason. Once, after falling asleep on the sofa, my husband had woken up to find himself standing in that tiny room in the pitch dark. Blind, he had screamed himself hoarse and clawed at the walls, the tendrils of roots brushing between his fingers, fearing he had somehow been buried alive. That Christmas, I stashed the gifts on the uppermost step of the rickety wooden stairs, knowing the children would never look there, and returned Christmas Eve to find them gone. Rats, my husband said, they'll eat anything. We laid traps, and the traps disappeared too.

After that miserable Christmas, in which we'd been forced to gift our children cheap consolation prizes, we closed the stolid wooden door and bolted it shut. We did not discuss it. There was simply nothing down in that room we wanted or needed, hence, no cause to venture down there again. Of course, these were the naïve pre-war days. Once the sirens began their wailing on a nightly basis, and there were sounds of percussive strikes on the horizon, we stopped thinking of the unpleasantness of unused rooms, the silly fear of inexplicable things, and began making a rudimentary shelter in the basement. The room did not run the length of our house. It was a design decision that confounded my husband and nulled its usefulness as anything other than a hiding space. Not a basement, but a nook. Perhaps, he said, it had been abandoned before they'd had a chance to finish it. It was the only thing that made sense, and though the wooden braces supporting all four walls suggested the job had been completed to the architect's satisfaction, I did not feel compelled to argue. By then, it hardly mattered.

April 20th, soldiers at the door instructed us to go down into the shelter and stay there. They were ashen faced, their eyes large and glassy, and did not seem possessed of the kind of bravery necessary to emerge victorious from the fray. It hardly instilled hope. Though bound to protect the citizens, many of them seemed more inclined to join them in their shelters or run far away from the danger. I could hardly blame them. With some blankets to protect against the frigid cold down below, and some bottles of water, a loaf of bread and a wedge of cheese, we hurried into the basement and pulled the door shut behind us, the air sirens already yowling at our backs.

Only this time, they did not stop.

The bombs fell after midnight.

The sound was like all the engines of the world breaking down at once, or as if a locomotive had been dropped from the sky. The human ear is not designed to process such cacophony, and as one we winced, our hands clamped to the sides of our heads.

The roar made of a mockery of my husband's whispered assurances, sucked the life from his words. As if he were an expert in such things, he quickly changed tactics, began to speculate loudly about which part of the town the bombs might have fallen. "That's probably the barracks," he said. "Or maybe the port." Pointing out that those two locations were at opposite ends of the town would have accomplished nothing, so I stayed silent, listened to the drone of the aircraft, the whistling of the bombs, the pounding of the explosions. Vibrations carried through the dirt walls, shuddering our organic unit. The children were wrapped around us, their heads buried in the folds of our clothes, dampening them with their tears. They wept soundlessly. My husband jolted with each explosion, his voice high and reedy. I could smell the whiskey on his breath but did not, as was customary, resent him for it. When the world wants to kill you, a bottle is as good a place to hide as a basement.

"Jesus Christ in Heaven," he said. "We forgot the gas masks. I should go get them."

"You'll do no such thing," I told him, and refrained from adding that if a bomb fell close enough to do us harm, it wasn't likely to be the gas that killed us.

More explosions, thunder through the walls, and dirt rained down from the ceiling. My daughter screamed into my stomach. My son buried his face deeper into my husband's shirt. The dozen or so candles we had set around us in a crude semicircle fluttered, sending shadows carousing around the room.

"They might be getting closer," my husband said. "But we'll be okay. We'll be safe down here."

I looked at him, glad he was here with us, but struck by how unfamiliar he appeared in his fear. Previously I had only ever known him as a strong man, determined, capable but not altogether liberal with his emotions, particularly love. He was a good father and kind, but often I could see when he was too tired or unwilling to handle the demands of the job. Dependent on the light on a given day, I sometimes detected shreds of lost dreams in his eyes, the vestigial traces of squandered ambition and goals unattained. We did not marry for love, but we had found the threads of it over time, mostly through the children that had necessitated our formal union. And now, here, on what might be the end of the world, I found his fear humanized him in a way his love never could, maybe because there was no doubting its legitimacy.

Another violating thrust as another bomb penetrated the city. More dirt rained on our heads. One of the candles went out. The room shook, and I held my daughter tighter to my chest. Her fingers were claws, nails drawing blood from my sides. I did not tell her to ease off, would have let her crawl inside me if it meant she'd be safe.

"We'll be okay," my husband said again. "We'll be okay."

I did not believe him. He had ceased his speculation about the location of the strikes, because they were getting closer, the last sounding as if it had hit a few streets away to the east. I looked away from him, the evident fear on his face only exacerbating my own, and straight ahead into the dark beyond the small arc of candles. There, I saw a pale smudge of something illuminated in the guttering flame, like a crooked stripe of paint on the opposite wall. Candle-shadow animated it, made it twist in on itself like a dash of milk in water. Perhaps the wall was crumbling. It filled me with dread that instead of the quick mercy of death from a sudden explosion, we might instead slowly die from suffocation as the walls gave way and the ceiling came down, choking us with dirt.

Further movement, this time closer to the floor, nearer the candles. My labored imagination and the poor light told me it was a spider, though I had never seen one quite so large. The splintered nails at the tips of its feet as it approached the flame told me I had been foolish in seeing it as anything other than a gnarled hand. My spine went rigid with shock, even as I reminded myself that now, under the existential stress of potential annihilation, I was likely to see and imagine anything from hands to enemy soldiers materializing from those walls.

"All right now," my husband said, hushing the anguish from our son. "Everything will be—"

The bomb that hit was not direct, as I would discover later. It hit the houses across the street from us, leveling most of that row, but the impact blew out our windows and most of the front wall, turned our furniture to splinters and collapsed the ceiling. Everything on the second floor tumbled down into the first, caving in the rabbit hutch the soldiers had assured would protect us in the event of such a calamity. None of the protective measures would have saved us, and I found myself thinking back to the reaction from one of the soldiers, little more than a boy, who had shaken his head at the mention of us remaining in our homes. "Unless you have an exterior shelter, it's better to leave than take the chance," he'd said. "Otherwise it'll be like trying to stop a tank with an umbrella." But this was our home. We could not afford to leave the city even if we'd had someplace else to go. And always that nagging doubt that the country was overreacting to verbal threats that would yield no physical retaliation. We were stubborn, and we stayed, held in place by some atavistic notion that we were merely caught in a dream from which we would inevitably awake before it could hurt us.

As the house above us fell, a cascade of dirt from the basement ceiling buried us from the waist down. The wall at my back crumbled, not completely, but enough so that I found myself reclined into a hollow, my mouth full of roots. Roots that seemed to move, fumbling like worms against my cheeks and eyes and between my lips, though that was most likely my own frantic attempt to be free of the concavity. Through the fall of dirt, I saw my husband bend over and clutch our son harder, and despite the madness, I felt a swell of love and gratitude for him, made myself a solemn promise to whomever might have the power to grant salvation, that if I survived, I would try to love him more, even if he was not emotionally capable of reciprocity.

I grabbed onto my daughter's frail quivering shoulders and screamed in anguished protest at the war, at the insanity of it all, and tasted coarse dry dirt on my tongue and in my throat. Why? I raged. Why us when we had done nothing to anyone but live our lives in a country that had challenged another? We were not the authority, the instigators. We were not the antagonists, but the spectators, the people in other rooms who only heard the mumblings of discontent through the walls. Why should *we* die? A lifetime of struggling, of trying to get by, undone in a heartbeat as a punctuation mark to a disagreement among strangers.

The hail of dirt subsided; the rumbling ceased. Other than the occasional sound of something shifting in the remains of the rooms above, it was quiet. My ears rang. It would be some time before I could hear properly again.

Only a single candle had endured the fall of dirt and dust. It guttered, appeared to die, then returned to cast its meager light through the haze. And in that feeble light, I saw a woman sitting against the opposite wall. I gave an involuntary gasp. She was no more than six feet away, but the light and the dust rendered her indistinct. Her crooked posture suggested injury, her eyes and mouth mere black thumbprints of shadow in the dirty gray egg of her face. I had the impression of an old print dress swaddling an oddly shaped body. She was sitting, her feet pointing toward the stairs. One foot was upside down, the toes buried in the floor. Her head faced in the opposite direction, turned slightly away from us. There were strange folds in the flesh of her neck. The bomb must have twisted her and flung her across the street and down here with us.

Dirty air rushed into the room from the holes in the ceiling.

I alerted my husband. It took him some time to hear me. When he looked at me, I saw that there was a nasty gash running from between his eyes up into his hairline. It was bleeding furiously down onto his shirt. He blinked rapidly and smiled at me with dirt-darkened teeth. "We're going...to be...okay," he said, and looked down at our son. The boy, lying half in the dirt, looked up at him, his eyes watery with panic.

I looked back into the dark.

The woman had moved and now her face and upper body were facing the wall. Her lower body had not changed position. Her feet were still pointed toward the stairs. But now her arms were raised, broken hands hanging loosely at shoulder height as if she were attempting some strange interpretation of an Egyptian dance. From the wall around her, more dirt tumbled as other hands began to worm their way through into the basement.

Rescuers? I wondered, and then I was being shaken violently enough to make my teeth clack together. Confused, I looked at my husband. He was very close and snarling at me. He must have gone mad. He was shaking me, then shoving me, then pulling our daughter out of my arms. Her nails dragged more furrows in my flesh. She was not moving. Her mouth was open and full of dirt. Wet warmth trickled from my nose. I brought a hand up to probe it and saw that I was holding the knife I had brought to cut the bread.

I mouthed questions into the darkness. No one answered.

I looked to the lady sitting by the far wall and saw that she had moved again. She was kneeling before me now, weaving slightly, using her weight to force her broken neck to bring her head around to where she needed it. Trying to face me.

My husband screamed in anguish. I dared not look. He was gesticulating wildly above the inert body of our daughter.

With a grunt, the old lady's head swiveled around to regard me, allowing me to see that her labors had been in vain. Somebody had stitched her eyes shut with black shoelaces. Her mouth too, but not tightly enough to deny her a smile.

My husband lunged at me, his hands hooked into claws. I saw that he was screaming but heard nothing but the ringing in my own ears and the very faint sound of the old lady's laughter.

Over her shoulder as my husband's hands found my throat, I saw that our son had crawled into the corner away from the chaos. From the dirt wall, a multitude of hands reached for him like plants drawn to the light.

"If you wish to see them, close your eyes," said the old woman.

I did as she requested, imagined what it would feel like to never have to open them again, and felt the old lady's hand guide my own, guide the knife, up and toward my husband's neck.

The next bomb reduced the house to rubble.

* * *

The shelling continued for three more days.

The basement withstood it all, only coming down at the behest of the rescuers' picks and shovels.

By that time, I had gone quite mad with grief and horror and sorrow. They took me to a mobile hospital and treated my injuries, most of which were superficial. In soothing tones, people—whether doctors, soldiers, or something else, I'll never know—informed me that my husband and two children had yet to be found. They advised me not to give up hope. Quite the contrary, they said. If the bodies were not in the basement, then it was quite likely they'd escaped and would find their way home in due course. But these people know nothing of errant Christmas presents and rat traps, of broken bodied old women with stitched up eyes, and of pale clambering hands bursting from the walls. Despite the authority in their voices, they are quite ignorant indeed.

They released me a week later, and I walked through a metropolis of debris, of fire and smoke, of pain and misery, of fear and confusion, to find my home. I missed it twice and had to backtrack. Home is harder to find when its face has been removed. Once I located the ruin in which I had married and raised my children, some kindly men assisted me in clearing some of the rubble that had fallen since my rescue, exposing for me the now exposed basement. I thanked them, dismissed their advice to stay clear, and clambered my way into the remains of that square of dirt. The walls were gone. Only the floor remained. The candle was there too, and I lit it with one of the three items I had taken from the hospital.

In the dirt, I sat and waited until the street and the city fell silent.

The moon rose high above my ruin, casting a patchwork of shadows on my face as the old woman's voice echoed through the feverish chambers of desperate memory.

"If you wish to see them, close your eyes."

From my pocket, I produced the other two items I had brought: a needle and some black thread.

She whispered to me of history, and of the future, and of holes blown in the earth by uneducated men, of broken prisons and freedom, and of old ones come again. She whispered to me of pain.

While I worked, and when it was time, the old lady's hand grew like a weed from the bloodied dirt before me and pinched out the candle flame.

By then, I didn't need the light.

DOWN HERE WITH US

I AM AWAKENED FROM A DREAM OF FIRE AND OLD BLOOD by a whisper. These days, it does not take much to rouse me, for despite the promised security of the wall, my instincts remain as sharp as ever. Maybe we are safe, and those instincts are little more than restless voices desperate to be heard, but they make me feel better whenever the light is gone from the day and the terrible moans of the Dead slip through the cracks in that wall.

"Olta, are you awake?"

I consider feigning sleep, but if anyone knows my instincts better than I do, it's my brother, as he should. He shares them, both of us cut from the same cloth as our father, even if I'm the only one who lived up to his promise. Thus, with a sigh I roll over to face where he is hunkered down next to my pillow. I wince at the stench of sweat and ale and onions that wreathes my face.

"What is it, Admir? And what time is it?"

"I have something to you show you, brother."

It seems as if Admir always has something to show me. He is younger than I by ten years, and truth be told, as naïve as a newborn. Every day his discoveries get more redundant and tiresome. Here is the remnant of an old shield half-buried in the mud; there, a well rumored to have no bottom, but from which he swears he can hear the ancestral prayers of the ashen priests. And oh, look, a half-mad Menhada woman who seems to be unaware that her shriveled breast is exposed.

"I've never had call to question your Great Father's sense," my comrade Ilion once remarked, "until I watched your brother for more than a minute. Then I found myself wondering why he didn't just drown that one in the brook."

To which I'd responded: "The water would have refused him."

"What is it?" I ask my brother again, suddenly more tired than I have any cause to be. We were warriors once, the greatest warriors in all the land, bested by no one, merely scarred by upheavals that would have reduced others to ash. We earned our wounds and our reputations, our pride. We earned the kingdom we built. Now we are weakened by immobility, by the lack of a cause to fight, by indignity and humiliation, and every day we struggle to find things to do, to find worth amid the bitterness of being *owned*.

Elldimek, our kingdom, which they have christened The Redoubt, belongs to another now, their only advantage against us being their greater number, an advantage that will do them little good when the world falls again. And it will, for though few dare to say it, the stench of carrion already so prevalent in the air seems to thicken with each passing day. Even the moons seem duller, as if the stink of death has tainted their light.

Something is coming, and in my most beautiful dreams, I imagine opening those doors again as my father once did, this time not to usurpers, but to devourers, a tactical move which would finally bring us all back down to the same level: that of meat.

"You'll have to come see. I don't have the words to describe it."

"Try."

His thickly bearded face scrunches up in concentration. I had hoped his education, crude as it is, would have taken root by now, but alas, I fear it's wasted on him. Not that this is a surprise. He thrives on stories that need no embellishments and yet get convoluted and more preposterous in the retelling with every passing season. And the Redoubt library, once the bastion of our ferocious history, has become tamed by the influence of other races. Now, instead of a shrine to dwarven pride, it has become an argument in which too many voices strain to be heard.

"I went outside," he says, much too loudly and in an instant, I am sitting up, my hand clamped over his mouth, surprising him. I take in the rest of the room, a one-time stable for our regal mounts that still smells of horse manure; a not unpleasant smell, if not for the implication that this is where we belong in the absence of other animals.

My comrades, two dozen in all, sleep on, enwombed by the amber dance with shadow beneath tallow flames.

"You went...*outside?* Have you gone mad?"

I remove my hand, repulsed by the feel of his spittle-soaked lips against my palm as he smiles.

"I wasn't alone. Nderin went with me. He's the one who told me about the garden in the woods. He'd been there before, with the Foresters. Only it was different then. There weren't so many of them."

Nderin is my friend Uril's son. Uril comes from a long line of butchers and you can still see in his eyes how much he wishes the meat were still pleading for mercy and dressed in the colors of our one-time enemies. His son is trouble enough that it is only a matter of time before the Dead get their hands on him. Never aloud would I admit it, but nobody would grieve if they did. And based on how he treats him, I suspect Uril feels the same. The blood that runs sluggishly through our veins has seldom felt so cold.

"You were warned not to go out there."

"Nderin knows a path. In the dark the Dead couldn't see us. And there are not nearly as many as before. You've heard the talk. There's rumors they might be going away."

"Talk is all that is and you're a fool to listen to it. Last time our people made benevolent assumptions, we ended up as slaves. Guessing at the patterns of the Restless is a good way to get yourself killed, or worse."

"The path is safe."

"Safe is not a word anyone gets to use anymore, Admir."

He wasn't listening, his eyes sparkling with excitement. "We only saw a few dozen of them, and the garden, it's hidden among the dead trees."

"What kind of garden?"

"You'll have to come see."

"You're a bigger imbecile than I thought if you think I'm going to go wandering out there in the dark to see some flowers."

"They're not flowers, though. That's the thing."

I lay down and roll away from him, close my eyes though I know he has ruined the notion of rest for me for another night. "Get some sleep. You have horseshit to shovel in the morning."

He sighs his frustration, puts a hand on my shoulder. "Please."

"I'll break your nose for you if you don't go to bed, Admir."

A grunt and he moves away, retreating to his cot, where, like the child I know him to be, he pouts and huffs until mercifully his dreams take him back to battlefields he can hardly recall.

In that, we are birds of a feather.

* * *

For the second time in as many hours I am dragged from sleep. Incensed, I am instantly ready to make good on my threat to shatter the cartilage in my idiot brother's nose, but upon opening my eyes to the first harsh strains of daylight through the rents in the stable roof, it is not Admir that stands over my cot, but Uril the Butcher. I know by the look on his long haggard face that there's trouble. Silently, I rise and get dressed, sparing a moment to sit on the edge of my cot, his presence like a thrummed violin beside me. My back aches, muscles sore.

"How long?" I ask him, lacing up my boots.

"Since last night."

"We should leave them to whatever fate befell them."

Uril, never a man to waste a word, merely nods in acknowledgment, but it's a redundant gesture. The fact that he's here and I am getting dressed means we've already made the decision to go after our fool kin. And I know why. Loyalty to one another, no matter how misguided, is all we have left, and our numbers are hardly so impressive we can afford to see them reduced, though the fact that Admir and Nderin have been gone since midnight does not augur well for their chances of survival.

To say nothing of our own.

I rise and look at Uril's shabby armor, the boiled leather so inadequate for his bulk it makes it difficult for him to breathe. I have the opposite problem with my own. These past few months, as food has become scarcer, I have lost weight and my armor hangs loose, reducing its efficacy. Soon it'll be an instrument of music, not war.

"We should speak to Behar."

Uril gives a single shake of his head and pats his belly, which tells me he has already anticipated the request and taken care of it. Which is wise. The less time we waste engaged in noxious verbal jousting with one of the Nightcoats, the better. As we are not permitted blades, we have, on our infrequent excursions beyond the wall, been forced to seek the aid of Karzhaddi and his thugs. Such arrangements are frequently unpleasant, costly, and best avoided, but one might say the same of death, which is, as any fool knows, the likely result of venturing outside unarmed.

Most of our brethren sleep on around us, as they will continue to do until the house master or his emissary comes and assigns them their tasks for the day. I am still in Dhimiter's service, but since his health has started to fail (at an alarming rate), he has been much less vigilant in keeping us in line. If we are still slaves, it is to our own memories and shame, and not because Dhimiter is in any way a governing force. He exits his house less and less these days, and on the rare occasions in which he is visible in daylight, his skin has a papery, translucent look. One wonders how long it will be before Rasuk and his master in the Undertaking come for him. Dhimiter has never been unkind, nor will he be missed. That he has any dominion at all (that *anyone* has) is an affront that will never be forgiven, only avenged when the wheel turns again.

We head outside into the morning sun, the smell of fresh cut grass a sensory illusion of serenity. It is nothing more than the scent of the lamps, which burn only at night for regulated hours, but permeate the day in the Downs.

Uril bows his head and does his best to ignore the curious looks of the helpless. Hollow-eyed wraiths watch us with envy only because we have not fallen *quite* so low. Filth runs in clotted brown rivers down the streets and there is waste everywhere. If it cannot be eaten, it lays discarded alongside those who have been discarded themselves. Once-proud people, thieves, respected politicians, murderers, valiant warriors—all have been made the same by poverty or punishment, and all of them reek of horror. Human, elf, dwarf, and ghûl, no matter what the race, they seem to gather closer together with each passing day despite having nothing to say, as if wretchedness wishes to stitch them together into one tragic tapestry.

Or as if they are becoming a single sentient entity out of fear of what's coming.

The Outer City stinks of death and decay. The perpetual presence of crows overhead, sometimes almost thick enough to block out the sun, fills me with foreboding. At least today we are spared the horrible sounds of the Dead beyond the wall. All is curiously quiet out there, but I am hardly encouraged by the silence. There was little noise the day my father opened the gates to our oblivion, either. I am reminded of this as Uril and I stand before them and the sentries go about facilitating our egress. There are others here—Foresters, farmers, and fools among them—eager to be the ones who return from their adventures with food and supplies... the currency of respect. They will fail, of course. There is nothing out there for anyone, anymore. I suspect even the Dead know that now, know that they've won, and that all they need to do is wait it out and we will join their ranks from the inside. Maybe that's why they've been so quiet.

A watchman atop the tower gives the all-clear. I hear one of the human sentinels mutter something about "a few less mouths to feed." Cranks turn, gears grind with a ferocious shriek, rust flakes off the cogs, and the chains rattle to life. The doors open, a wooden mouth yawning wide, bathing us in carrion breath. Out here the crows spot the landscape like black marks indicating the location of the fallen. And they are everywhere, some felled by the sentries, others the bodies of misfortunates exiled as punishment for crimes against the Magisterium.

Inside the wall are farms, houses, homes, as close to an ordinary existence as one can expect in the hell the world has become. There are also dungeons, sewers, tunnels, courts. But out here, there is nothing but dead earth, the grass trampled flat, the clay poisoned by the corrupted remains of the Restless. Fires razed the woods and the trees were twisted and stunted when they returned to life. It is a lifeless landscape, perpetually covered in an omnipresent mist that ebbs and flows like the ghost of a forgotten sea.

"Move along," barks one of the sentries, an unmistakable note of glee in his voice, and when I close my eyes, I imagine slipping the blade Ulric passed me up under his helmet and slicing his throat. It's a brief thought, but the imagined scent of fresh blood, the heat of it coursing over my fingers, stirs my loins.

And then we are outside, two dozen of us in all, and the gate slams shut with a finality that vibrates through my bones.

As one, wordlessly, we start to walk.

* * *

We hunted these lands once, brought animals down with unmatched skill and reveled in the kill with our brethren. Carcasses were dragged or carried over the shoulder home to our kingdom for ribald celebrations that would last until the sun rose, sometimes longer. The following day the streets would be populated by women and children who looked upon us adoringly (or with good-humored pity), as the hangover forced us to seek out the cure. All of that is gone now, stolen from us in a moment, and that world is nothing more than a thing of old stories and wistful memory. Our home is a prison, the streets crowded with wretches who no more recognize our worth than they do their own. And out here, our once-fair land reeks, the foul breeze like a diseased giant blowing upon his meal before devouring it.

All the animals are gone, either run to safer territory or wiped out entirely, for when the Dead could not get at us, they took what they could. We have even seen them eating clay, and each other.

We walk for an hour before stopping to rest, midway between home and the sprawling woods in which I spent the greater part of my childhood. Back when fighting the horde seemed like a sound strategy, we lit those woods aflame, watched it burn, the conflagration like the whole world burning as the Restless, who had been using it as a corridor, were cooked. Most considered it a victory, but for months I felt a hard knot of sadness in my throat at the thought of what we had done, of the beauty we had destroyed. Long before I learned to hunt, the woods had been my haven, a magical hiding place, a kingdom unto itself. There I learned to use my imagination to conjure up impossible monsters; I conquered them all like the mighty warrior I promised myself I would someday become. And I did, only to find myself shoulder-to-shoulder with my brothers as we razed that Place of Dreams. Slavery, sickness, grief... nothing has since eclipsed that loss for me. All of us have the day we knew our world was dead. That was mine.

Ever since, I have become a ghost in a land of ash.

As I sit upon a rock gnawing on a piece of stale bread and looking up at the jaundiced clouds, Uril taps a knuckle against my shoulder. I look up at him, a stone-faced monolith in armor, and he nods at something behind me, in the direction of the woods. The bread is like a stone that lodges in my throat as I rise.

Through the phalanx of blackened stems that is all that remains of the woods, one of the Restless comes, cerulean eyes like dull stars trapped in the black hole of its skull. It is horribly emaciated, practically indistinguishable from the spindly arachnidan trunks of the trees through which it moves with incongruous grace. And although nothing but vellum stretched tight over bones, it has somehow found the ability to smile.

I draw my dagger, but Uril stays my hand. There is a light in his eyes that I know all too well, and without speaking, his words are clear: *Allow me this one. There will be more.*

Once the dead thing has been dispatched, the blue light in its eyes remaining lit though its head has been removed, we stand in silence for a moment. At length, spurned by the frustration of inactivity, the quiet is broken as the Foresters take their own path, bound for the hills to the east and to land they hope has been neglected by the attention of the desperate Dead. There are fourteen of them. Only luck will preserve that number when they return. On each of their faces is acknowledgment of this fact. On most, the fear is tempered by apathy. We have lived long enough. We bid them safe passage with unspoken blessings, then watch as another, smaller group heads off to the west and to the plains. I trust no one in this group. They are dwarves but have managed the admittedly enviable task of forgetting where they came from. If they are slaves, the Nightcoats hold the deed, and as such, the nature of their mission outside the walls will go unknown by all but those within the cabal.

Which leaves only four: me, Uril, and the two young dwarves, Tarek and Veli, who seem to have ventured outside the gate simply for the fun of it, or as a break from the misery that exists within. For them, we have little patience. It is the foolishness of youth that has brought us here, after all. As Uril heads straight on through the woods, I turn to look at Veli, the younger of the two, as he tussles with his friend.

"You."

He stops dead as if I have slapped him. I have always been intimidating in aspect, at least among my own kind, but these days the black hate that exists in my skull has made oil of my eyes. I have seen them reflected in glass and it frightens even me.

"Yes?"

"You were a fool to come," I tell him, and then glance at Tarek. "Both of you. And you are not our charges. If you should fall behind or fall prey to another, we will leave you, so you have a choice: stay close or head home. Do you have weapons?"

Veli produces a sharpened stick.

Tarek brandishes a long thin needle, no doubt stolen from his mother's knitting basket.

I can see by their faces that until this moment, they believed themselves aptly armed, which they are if they also continue in the belief that the Dead have receded, a belief in my soul I know is wrong. The stench of them fills my nose, carried to me on a breeze that has come from darker places.

The boys can see by my face that they have made a mistake.

Tarek stares at his feet.

Veli clears his throat. "We will stay close, Olta. We will watch your back."

For this, he earns more respect from me than I let show. Weaker men would have run. I turn and join Uril, who has just entered the woods like a knife through the ribcage of some enormous beast.

* * *

It is not the world of my childhood within those blackened bones, but the world as it is now: a graveyard. Death and old smoke cloy my nostrils as I follow Uril's lead through the charred stalks of the trees. The ground beneath our feet is thick and loamy but crunches here and there as burnt wood and bark are driven further into the earth. A bluish haze hangs in the air, as if the last fog got caught in the maze. A brief glance over my shoulder shows the boys following silently, the color drained from them by my words and the mist both. Their faces have hardened now, annoyed perhaps that they allowed themselves to forget their nobility, their pride, the instinct that should govern everything to keep them alive. But they are young and part of a new generation that no amount of teaching can make whole. Those days are gone. Assuming they live to grow older, they will be pretenders, shadows of what our race once was and can never be again.

A sudden burst of noise and my head snaps back around, my body tensing into a defensive posture, blade extended, breath held. I look up. The sickly clouds are momentarily eclipsed by a multitude of crows as they screech ahead of us, bound for whatever lies ahead. Their numbers seem endless, the cacophony the only sound in the world.

What do you know? I ask them. *What do you see?* Would that we could harness their flight, their sight, their wisdom, then perhaps we might stand a chance in the war to come. As it stands, we are merely waiting for the inevitable end.

It takes minutes, hours, weeks, for the last stragglers to pass over our stilled quartet. The noise recedes. Even still, I listen, for the crows are omens and it will do us well to measure the distance it takes them to reach where they're going, to reach the instruments of our doom. That there is something out there is not in question, only where it is and how long it will take to reach us, to reach Elldimek.

I straighten, look back at the boys and note that the mist has thickened into a fog around us. "Come."

They narrow the gap between us in an instant and look up at me breathlessly, awaiting my command. In Tarek's eyes I see the slightest spark of defiance and bitterness. It is a quality I admire. If he can learn to harness it, make a fire from all those unruly sparks, there might be hope for him, yet.

"Stay close but keep an eye on our backs. I'd rather not have any surprises."

As one the boys nod, Veli's gaze lingering a moment longer than necessary before he moves away, as if he was trying to read something in my face. He won't, of course. The people who might have been able to divine meaning from my eyes are long since buried. At the thought, I touch the spot on my breastplate where my wife's silver ring used to hang from a cord around my neck. It is, like so many things, gone now, adorning the finger of another who knows nothing of our love or the anguish which stains that ring. I traded it to avoid starving, to keep death away a moment longer, as I couldn't keep it from her. Maybe if the balance turns again, I'll have an opportunity to find it.

Such notions exist as fragile comforts in the moments before sleep.

For the first time since embarking on this fool's errand, I think of my brother. I have avoided it until now because with the summoning of his face comes awareness of his death. He is a warrior, yes, but a poor one, and I can only imagine, based on the excitement that limned his tongue last night, that battle was the furthest thing from his mind. There is a chance, of course, that he ventured out here and encountered nothing, but there's not a part of me that believes it. Out here is a hell in waiting.

I expect to find him dead, torn to pieces, or to not find him at all. There was a time when the absence of a body to bury would have haunted me. Not so any more. And should I find him dead, will I mourn his loss? Some part of me will, yes, as any man would lament the taking of kin, but things have changed too much for me to care as I should. He is little more than another body now, and one that has become a burden. The cruelest part of me anticipates the relief I will feel when I confirm he's gone, for so often it is akin to having a child in my care. With the world on the verge of change once more, I need to be unencumbered.

Ahead, Uril stops and leans forward. He has spotted something in the murky soup between the dead trees. At my approach, he raises a hand and I cease moving. Behind me, I hear the boys do the same. Then I realize my mistake. Not boys. *Boy.*

I start to turn, and a crow explodes toward me from somewhere between the trees to my left. It does not feel like a merry coincidence; it feels intentional, part of a design that will have many parts and leave me in a similar state when it ends. I raise an arm over my face as the crow skims close enough for me to feel the displaced air as he caws and swoops upward. *The crows are their familiars.* Then he is gone, his darkness stitched back into the shadows that birthed him and I am turning again, scanning the graveyard of bones for the boys and finding only one.

Veli stands a few feet away, his back to me. I spare a moment to check on Uril. He is still in the same place, as rooted to the ground as the trees, but upon sensing my attention, looks reluctantly away and meets my gaze. Then he looks beyond me, toward Veli, and his face changes, goes slack. It is not an expression I have ever seen before, and it fills me with foreign dread.

I follow his gaze back to Veli, who is where I left him, but now the boy's body is quaking so violently it's as if he's being manhandled by a ghost. He is close enough for me to grab him if I'm willing to move, but for the moment I can't, and it is not quite fear that holds me in thrall, but awe. Awe at the thing I have mistaken as the movement of dead branches through the fog. It is nothing so benign, and for all I have seen in my time in this world, I am aware that I am bearing witness now to something that will change me from this moment forth.

It is taller than any of the Restless we have seen thus far. Taller than three men, and no part of it is thicker than my wrist. It looks for all the world like an effigy made animate, a crude idol of rope and bone. A gathering of sticks. And as it ducks low and pulls itself through the narrow gap between the boles of dead trees, it appears as if the woods itself has given birth to it. The fog whirls away at its approach, allowing me the full view of the horror it represents here in this dreadful place. Nothing about it suggests anything human, but there are features twisted and buried beneath its bark-like skin, a mottled face, as if a man died and was subsumed by a withering tree, granting it some form of perverse life, threading its veins with sap. Its chest heaves as it draws itself back up to full height and now that it has shredded the fog that obscured it from view, I can see that in its right hand hangs the limp body of Veli's friend, Tarek. The head and one arm are missing, the stumps squirting blood down onto the blackened earth, slaking its thirst. The creature's jaw moves languidly as he chews on the boy's remains.

Perhaps to compensate for his embarrassment, to prove his worth and impress, Tarek decided to seek out the source of a noise, and in so doing, sealed his fate.

I look down at my hand, at the blade. It may as well be a feather for all the good it will do. I dare cast another glance at Urik. He is frozen by fear, as he should be. Bravery has found an inhospitable home here. If we fight, we will die. If we run, it will follow, but of these two choices, only the latter makes sense. It is not my time. Not yet. I will know it when it comes, but it does not come today, not at the hands of this godless devil of sticks and bone and rope and blue fire in place of eyes.

"Urik," I hiss, and hear a creaking sound as the creature ceases its masticating and turns in my direction. I watch it cock its triangular head toward my voice. Blind. Despite the twin blue orbs of fire, the thing has no eyes. Urik brings his wide gaze to bear on me.

I tilt my head toward the trees at our back. "We run." He nods once and some of the life, if not the color, returns to his face. Sometimes the mere thought of action can draw a man out of himself and away from certain death.

"The boy," he whispers. "Don't let the Witherer take him."

He has just christened this creature. Henceforth, this is how it shall be known. Not some nameless thing, as it deserves to remain, but *The Witherer*, a name that will instill fear in all who hear it, for it, like so many of this creature's ilk, portends a quick yet painful end, an abomination that has no right to be here and now has dominion. Its presence confirms that we do not know what roams the territory beyond our walls, that we have been arrogant in thinking our enemy familiar. The terrible truth is that we know less than we did before.

The world has gone mad.

In two quick steps I have the boy by the scruff of the neck.

"No!" he screams, mistaking me in his fright for another devil of the woods.

And that is all it takes for the Witherer to find us.

The sound of it lunging toward us is the sound of all the kindling in the woods breaking at once, and I do not wait to feel the twigs of its fingers on my body. I am gone, running, dragging the young one flailing along with me through the fog. I have no idea where I am going, only that behind us is death so I must keep pushing ahead. More than once my progress is halted by trees, the pain of the collision setting stars alight in my eyes, in my bones, but I persevere, Urik a bulky shadow to my left, keeping the pace. The brush crashes down behind us, trunks are pulverized, groan and fall. The Witherer comes, stalking us through the same woods where I became a warrior before burning them down just as this creature would burn me down, and perhaps I deserve it after all. Perhaps this thing is not Restless. Perhaps it has been resting all along and the woods have resurrected it to make me pay for my desecration of this sacred place.

Perhaps it is an end I deserve. And in that moment, I think not of my brother, of my brethren, of anything but moving forward and away from that hellish demon that would strip me of my skin. I am not afraid to die.

I am afraid to die and become Restless.

Veli's foot finds a root and he is yanked from my grasp as surely as if the Witherer snatched him away. I slow but do not stop, glance back at the dazed boy struggling to his feet, and I think of going back for him, think of being brave, of trying to save him. But then instinct takes over and I know that if I do not stop, do not go back, the boy will be killed, and the killing and the feeding will slow the creature down. The boy will die; we will live. I do not enjoy making this decision. There is no nobility in it, only self-preservation. But the choice is made, and I run and close my eyes as the crashing sounds behind me abruptly cease and the boy's scream shatters the brief silence until it too is made silent.

Urik is still with me, a shadow in the fog, and I wonder what he will say, what he will think, and then realize I don't care. He will thank me for his life, as I thank Veli for mine. Should we live to recount this tale, there will be no mention of the forced sacrifice, of my abandonment of the child. These are not details that will matter to anyone but the parents, and even their grief will be muted by the fear of what we have encountered in the dead woods today.

We run for an hour, until we are certain the only sounds we can hear are those of our own passage, the thunder in our chests and ears and throats, and still we do not stop.

Only when the fog is gone and the light returned to the day do we rest, in what appears at first glance as a clearing. What it resolves to be upon closer inspection is, in some ways, worse than the thing behind us.

Urik looks at me. "We should go home."

I agree, but not yet, partly out of curiosity, mostly because I know he is trying to protect me from what I might see.

We have reached not a clearing, but a garden, ringed so perfectly by the trees it looks as though it was designed by man and not nature. But though this is undoubtedly the garden of which my brother spoke, nothing grows here... though plenty has been planted.

"We should go," Urik says again, his impatience marked by renewed terror at the new atrocity laid out before us.

It is a garden of hands, of arms buried in soil. Dozens of them, each one reaching into the air like some strange kind of fleshy plant. Each one sprouts from the elbow, and though there is nothing to suggest that these limbs have not been severed from their owners, I know this is not true. I know there are bodies beneath the blackened earth.

"Why?" Urik asks. "Why would someone do this?"

I can only shake my head. It is not a question that is likely to ever be answered, and in truth I care less about the genesis of this terrible display than I care about finding out who populates it. And after a half-hearted attempt to dissuade me Urik turns back to guard our backs, his eyes set on the fog as it recedes like a sheet pulled away from a corpse. For now, the woods appear empty back there. If we are fortunate, the Witherer has retreated to feed on the bounty it took from us.

I walk among the hands, out for a stroll in a garden of Hell. Whomever interred these poor creatures did not distinguish by race. There are humans here, and dwarves, even an elf. It looks like a mockery of the dead woods around us, all those hands twisted into claws, grabbing at the air in desperation as they died, suffocating, their lungs filled with dirt.

It does not take me long to find what I'm looking for, and as if he has been waiting for it, as if this was the real reason he didn't want me among the arms, Urik turns to look at me, his face grim.

The arm reaching from the dirt before me has an inked symbol of a wolf on its blanched white wrist, courtesy of the street people who offer such things in trade. Such practices are common, but the street people pride themselves on never repeating a design.

And this one belongs to Nderin, Urik's son.

At the look in my eyes, he nods his acceptance of the news and trudges through the dirt to where I stand. I put a hand on his shoulder and leave him to his mourning, though I suspect it will be quiet and not long. Urik has never had much love for his son. If anything, he has seen him as a disappointment, which I have often suspected is simply us looking at our kin as mirrors, but like me, loyalty has brought us here to retrieve them, alive or dead.

I search the remaining graves, if such a name can be employed for this wickedness, and although my brother is not marked, I will recognize his stubby fingers.

But he is not here.

Urik jolts and takes a step back just as I am sitting down to smoke upon a moss-shrouded rock. Pipe to my mouth, match held aloft, I look and forget the fire until it burns my fingers.

The hand next to Ndemir's has moved. Then his son's hand moves.

Then they all do.

"Olta..." Urik shakes his head. "Could they be...?"

I shake my head. We have been here too long, and while my kind are known to be able to survive longer in situations in which others would suffocate, even we dwarves couldn't manage such a prolonged internment. Before the Witherer, we might have fooled ourselves into hoping that there's still a chance for Ndemir. Now it can only be more witchery, another display of the wicked magic that permeates this place. And we should not be here. Every moment brings us closer to our own destruction, a reality that is hardly limited by this place, but seems represented by it.

Urik starts to bend down to grab his son's hand. In a flash I am by his side, my hand clamped on his wrist. "No," I tell him. "Not unless you want to join him."

And as if they have heard, the hands grow still, underwater flowers in the absence of a current.

"Home," I say, and though it takes us an eternity, at last we move, not back the way we have come, but to the west, the long way around. We are willing to endure the protracted journey if it means we are free of this hellish place.

Urik the Butcher, Urik the Quiet, says nothing on the long walk home. He simply surveys the landscape and absently massages his wrist.

* * *

Some unknown time later, the walls of Elldimek hove into view, misted by distance. From here I can see the black specks of the crows. They are not circling but roosting on the walls. Watchers.

My feet ache, and my heart aches, too. I want to rest, but so close to home and unsure of what further surprises the Outside might have in store for us, I walk on. Urik trails behind. His is not a mask of sorrow, but anger, for though he might have little feeling left for Ndemir in his deadened soul, still he feels the theft of one of our own at the hands of these ungodly creatures. With it comes the awareness that this will never end, that we are the hunted now and one day the sun will rise on a world that is empty of natural life. Our kingdom, already stolen once, will be owned for good by demons, and we will be no more.

And perhaps that is how it should be, for what use are we to this world as slaves? Even those who would own us are themselves owned by the monsters that exist beyond the walls.

"Olta," Urik says, breathless. "Stop."

I do as he asks. He is bent double, bile unspooling from his mouth in a long silvery thread. I wait, watching him carefully as the foul breeze blows around us and the crows watch quietly. I consider this giant of a man, a man that in the old days fought proudly alongside me, a man I would have called a friend. Today, we are strangers. I have no money to buy his meat, and the Foresters don't provide enough to keep him in business, which renders him a butcher in name only. I no longer trust this man.

"Do you wish to share something with me before we reach the gate, Urik?"

He takes his time gathering his breath, clearing his lungs, and then he straightens, allowing me to see the blade in his hand. It is held downward, unthreateningly, but this offers little comfort, not given my suspicion of him, confirmation of which I have awaited since I first awoke to find him in my quarters.

There is nothing to read on his face.

"Why did you really bring me out here? Was it the Nightcoats?" I ask him.

He says nothing, betrays even less.

"Why?"

Still he is silent, but that is condemnation enough. "What benefit in killing me and my brother?"

He shakes his head, only slightly, but without words I cannot decide if he is denying my words or simply can't explain the motives behind his assignment.

"Are they simply weeding out the weak so their resistance will be stronger when the time comes?"

"Olta..."

"And what of your boy? Was that your test? Did they require a sacrifice before they could trust you? You didn't look upset enough to have found him in that garden."

"I don't—"

"Is that because you put them there? Was it you who buried all those people in the woods? Is it some kind of ritualistic burial ground? Help me to understand. Did you bring me there to kill me? Did you kill Admir, too? Where is he?"

He shakes his head again and now there is pain on his face. "It's not like that."

I step closer to him and his knife hand twitches. The crows rejoice. "Then what *is* it like? Why didn't you kill me in the woods?"

"Olta."

I wait, but there are no more words coming. Perhaps that is why he doesn't speak, because it is impossible for most people to speak without deception. A mute man can never be called a liar. But it also deprives us of the truth if there is a truth to be had.

"Were you planning to cut my throat before we were in full view of the gate? Or did you just intend to cripple me so that the Restless would take me and you would appear innocent of your crimes? Tell me, Urik, why have you turned on us, on your brothers? What have we done to you?"

His brow furrows. "Olta, I didn't—"

A shuffling sound behind him and he turns, knife raised. I close the distance between us and slip my own blade into his throat and twist, tug it upward and withdraw. Then I step away as Urik's head comes back around, his eyes like boiled eggs. He reaches for me, his hand clutching like that of his own murdered son in the garden. He chokes, sputters blood, winces, and then drops to his knees.

I watch him wheezing at my feet, blood spurting from the gash in his neck, and then I raise my eyes to the figure standing still and watching a few feet away from where he stood.

In truth, I do not know whether Urik betrayed me. It is possible, as all things are these days. The Nightcoats are gaining in strength. They whisper, build their existence atop a castle of secrets. That they have plans for Elldimek is not one of those secrets, only what the nature of those plans may be. They are cunning, ruthless, dangerous. And despite living within the confines of a stone prison, they yet make people disappear. I may never know if Urik was their emissary, or if I and my brother were truly targets. It is just as likely that I thirst for blood, that my discontent with the shadow my life has become has led me to take blood where I can find it, even if that means my own kind, even if I must falsely vilify them. In fighting the creature, in breathing this air, in seeing the woods, I recalled more than ever what it felt like to be a warrior. It is all I was ever meant to be, and without it I am a ghost... worthless, purposeless, a waste. As my father once said, "In the absence of other prey, a wolf will eat his own."

It pleases me to think myself a wolf.

Before me is the cub, my brother, weaving before me, exhausted, changed, covered in filth. His face is made of chalk, his mouth hanging slack.

"Olta? Oh, brother, thank God it's you."

As I near him, teeth clenched and blade at the ready, I see the blue fire in his eyes.

I am mad. I am whole.

I am a warrior.

SANCTUARY

"GO GET YOUR FATHER," MOTHER SAID, and the spoon froze a half-inch from Liam's milk-sodden lips. His gaze moved from the daydream he'd been projecting upon the wall above the scarred kitchen table, to his left, where his mother was laboring over the stove. The bacon and eggs were burning. He could smell them as they hissed and popped. His mother, almost skeletally thin beneath her threadbare robe, stabbed at them as a blue plume of smoke rose around her, or maybe *from* her. It was hard to say. It was, after all, Sunday morning, and he couldn't remember the last time he'd seen her be anything but angry on a Sunday.

Between his mother and the table stood an empty chair, where on any other morning, his father would have been sitting, face buried in a newspaper and communicating in mumbles. But as the sacristan, Father was required to go to church on Sunday, both services. Afterward, he celebrated spirits of a different kind.

With difficulty, Liam swallowed his cereal and lowered the spoon. His mother's request made him feel sick. He didn't want to get dressed, didn't want to walk through the snow down the narrow crumbling street. Lately it had begun to feel like a throat eager to ingest him. And most of all, he didn't want to go to McMahon's, the corner bar where he knew he'd find his father. He just wanted to finish his breakfast and go back upstairs to his room, to his sanctuary, where he spent most of his time reading and writing and drawing. It was safe there, surrounded by the portraits he had drawn to keep him company, portraits he wished were real so that they could take the place of the real world. Down here where the adults existed, there was nothing but raised voices and hurt feelings, infrequently punctuated by unexpected bursts of violence from which even he was not immune. Like the smell of those burning eggs, he felt the sourness and uncertainty of the world outside his room trying to attach itself to him like a second skin, trying to induct him into the same misery that had assimilated his parents.

"Won't he be back soon?" he asked his mother, quietly.

"Do what you're told," she snapped without turning to look at him, and that was good. As long as the coldness of her gaze was not on him, he could be brave, continue to make his case. As soon as she looked at him, she would kill the words in his mouth, and he would know he was doomed.

"The weather's really bad," he said, and glanced out the window. Beyond the frosted glass, thick snowflakes fell like feathers from a ruptured pillow. "He'll probably want to get home before it gets any worse."

He jumped as the spatula made a sharp clang against the side of the frying pan. "For fuck *sake*, Liam," she said in a dangerous voice, "If I have to ask you again, I'll put your head through the wall."

He rose quickly, careful not to let the legs of his chair scrape against the stone floor. His parents hated that. He didn't like it much either, but it's not like it was ever intentional. He cast a longing glance at the half-eaten bowl of soggy cornflakes and the slice of cold toast and marmalade sitting untouched next to it and went to get his coat and boots on. At the doorway, he looked back at his mother. Although he was only ten years old, he could remember a time when she didn't look so pale and faded, like a photograph left too long in the sun. There were still memories of her lit from within by the light of summer. He remembered her love. Now, as he looked upon a lank-haired witch glaring down into a frying pan full of blackened, twisted things, he feared he would never know that love again.

"And tell him if he doesn't come home, he can stay with whatever whore will have him," she said through an ugly sneer that made her face look like a cheap mask melting in the heat from the stove.

Silently, Liam exited the room.

* * *

Winter had made a monochrome gradient of the world, broken here and there by dark strips where the snow had fallen like flesh from the withered arms of the trees and the twisted remains of broken streetlights, which bent over the street like the bones of some long-dead giant. Liam was bundled up in a thick woolen jacket, but the holes he'd worn in the elbows allowed the icy wind to creep in, chilling him where he stood. Over his scarf, the wet wool sent bolts of discomfort through him whenever it brushed against his teeth.

He looked down at the path. The snow had all but erased his father's footprints, leaving only faint impressions behind.

A series of muffled thumps behind him. Liam turned around. The house was an old Cape Cod, as dilapidated as everything else in this part of the city: a squat dispirited structure, the gaps in the once-white siding so stained with green mold, it looked like the side of an old boat. The inverted triangle of his mother's vulpine face, contorted in anger, filled the kitchen window. Mercifully, the thick glass and the soughing of the wind immunized him from the poison of her words, but the jab of her finger made the message clear enough: *Get moving.*

Breath held, shivering for reasons other than the cold, he did as instructed and stepped off the stoop.

The snow reached his knees, which made traversing the short path to the street all that more difficult, but he was thankful for the delay. The world on this side of the chain-link gate may not have been a paradise, but it was still home, and home was where his sanctuary was: up the stairs and down the end of the hall. It may as well have been another country. That's where dreams were allowed; the nightmares stayed downstairs.

Aware without looking that his mother's eyes were on him, he trudged onward toward the gate.

* * *

The street was too narrow to allow the passage of vehicles, even if such a thing were possible, and the snow made it narrower still, which did nothing to alleviate Liam's impression of it as a gullet that would feed him into the ugly belly of the neighborhood. Once upon a time, this part of the city had thrived, an extension of the bustling metropolis that had long ago been rendered inaccessible by a wall of kudzu vines and weeds, which, almost unnoticed, had sprouted from the earth from between the remains of the old steel and grain mills before tearing them down and fortifying the wall. Before nature had reclaimed it, this had been a vital industrial outpost on the outskirts of the city, but with the death of industry and the departure of men whose aspirations ran further than drink, drugs, and murder, it had become a dead zone, a literal wrong side of the tracks, themselves buried beneath the tangles of blackened vine and twisted steel

To Liam's left, stood a rank of dead, blank-faced houses, their eyes lightless, the caps of their porch rooves pulled low as if in shame, open maws empty of anything but dust and dark. Discarded toys half buried by the snow made an incongruously colorful cemetery of the yards, rusted swing-sets like shriveled scale models of all that remained of the mills which had once served as the district's thriving heart.

To the right, a sharp decline led down to all that remained of the train tracks, the veins through which life had coursed through this outpost. In places, some unknown force had ripped the tracks up and twisted them back in on themselves. The gravel had long been scattered. Beyond, the land fell away, became an industrial wasteland masked by the drifts. Here there were no children building snowmen or throwing snowballs or sledding. Everything was quiet, everything was buried. This did not surprise Liam. It was, after all, a Sunday, and in places such as these, places in which all that's left is faith, Sundays meant reverence. Outward signs of joy not directly affiliated with the gods would have been considered an affront.

Liam shivered, the cold now deep within his bones, his hands chilled beneath the gloves. He welcomed the discomfort, however, for it kept him from thinking about what he had seen the last time his mother had forced him to fetch his father.

Open your mouth about this, Liam, and it'll be the last time you'll be able to.

The houses drifted silently by and his school hove into view. Liam hated the school almost as much as he hated church (though he would die before he'd admit such a thing out loud), the tavern, and the neighborhood itself. School was prison, the walls speckled with some foul-smelling mineral deposit that glowed blue in the halflight. The hallway floors were bowed upward as if they'd built it atop the back of a sleeping giant. Few of the classroom lights worked and the teachers all appeared as if they'd been raised from the dead: pallid, drawn, their voices those of people who have found themselves in some terrible dream. The bathrooms smelled of brine; the chalkboards appeared to ripple when written upon, as if made of tar. To anyone else, it would have been a thing from nightmare. To Liam, it was the place of his education, though as he grew older, he had started to question the catechisms and syllabi to which he was being exposed. They seemed antiquated and decidedly cruel.

The school was an enormous Italianate Victorian, the structure much too big for the two dozen or so students who went there, an anachronism whose façade seemed to suggest a smug awareness of its incongruity. The upper floors had been sealed off with strict warnings to all students not to trespass, which of course Liam had, and though he had found nothing but an endless series of faltering rooms stacked full of ancient books, he hadn't felt quite the same since. "The dust found its way inside me," he'd written on his sketchpad after returning home that day, but he had no idea what that was supposed to mean. He didn't even remember writing it or drawing the picture of the janitor with the arms growing out of his mouth. In one of the old man's hands, he had drawn an alarm clock.

Liam looked away from the school. At the far end of the neighborhood, barely visible through the blizzard, stood the church. Even from here it looked like a face with hollow, admonishing eyes and a gaping mouth, the head atop the body he was now traversing like a tick. As much as he feared the school, the church absolutely terrified him, for surely if this part of the city had a black heart, a source of all its hated life, it was there within the unnaturally thick walls of the crumbling church. His parents had raised him to pray, to revere the gods that dwelled inside that place, and, as he was a good child and afraid of parents and gods alike, he had obeyed, might have continued to do so if not for his mother.

It was a day he would never forget. The Day of Leaves. He had been sitting in his room, daydreaming, the pencil in his hand moving of its own accord, sketching. His mother had burst into the room and slammed the door behind her, startling him. Her nose was bleeding, and her eyes were wide. She looked like a wild thing, feral. It was the first time he had seen her look this way, but it wouldn't be the last. On that day, his body had tensed as she rushed toward him, but rather than strike or admonish the boy, she had grabbed him by the shoulders and brought her face close to his. Her breath had smelled sour, toxic, alien.

"You must listen to me, Liam," she'd said in a tone he wasn't sure he had ever heard before. Pleading, almost whining. "You must listen to your mother now, do you understand?"

Confused and frightened, he'd somehow managed a nod.

"Good, good. That's a good boy." She sat down next to him, her skin reeking of smoke and ash. Her hair was tangled, the edges singed. She kept pulling at it as she spoke. "I don't want you going to church anymore. I don't want you going anywhere your father goes, okay?"

"Okay," he'd said, because there was nothing else he could say.

"Promise me."

"I promise." Given his feelings on the subject, it was not a difficult promise to make. He appeared to be the only child not enthused by the prospect of further visits to a monstrous building that made his head hurt. He could have gone forever never smelling that sulfur smell again, or sitting on those mildewed pews, or looking upon the strange upside-down effigy with the goat's head someone had hung above the altar. He would be happy to never again hear the organ that only played tunes better suited to old ice cream trucks even when nobody was playing it. No, he would be perfectly happy to never set foot inside such a place again. Up until that moment, the only thing that had kept him from obeying his instincts in that regard had been his parents' intervention.

"You don't know what it is. What they're doing to us. What they've already done to your father. You must stay away from there and you must stay away from *him*. Do you understand?"

"Yes."

"You'll be safer in your room where nothing has to change."

"Okay."

She had shaken him one more time to be sure the words had reached him and then, satisfied, she did something she would never do again: she kissed him lightly on his brow. It burned where her lips had touched his skin. Then she was gone.

He thought that day might have been the last one in which his mother had shown him any love. Though there had been far better days in the beginning before they reopened the church and tore the light from the sky and the color from the world, he still considered the Day of Leaves a good one because she had still cared. She had even kissed him!

But soon the poison got to her too, changed her, and while she continued to resist—sometimes so much he could *feel* it radiating in warm waves from her skin—she was no longer the same woman now. It was only a matter of time before she started going to church again, and then she'd make him go too. And gods only knew how they would be made to pay for straying.

The school lurched away from him, an explosion of vines separating supposed innocence from the world of the adults. Here, propped atop cracked concrete sidewalks, was McMahon's, the town hall, The Elder's House, the police station, and finally Ned's Grocery Store. Stone facades leaked viscous fluid from the cracks; fungus hemmed the bottoms. The rooves had sunken in the middle as if under the weight of something enormous and unseen. The breeze tore wisps of smoke from the slanted chimneys. On the opposite side of the road, a six-foot high stone fence topped by wrought iron railings blocked the view of the marsh but not the turbulent motion of the phosphorescent air above it. Green and yellow lights pulsated within the miasma. Tall withered trees that had grown up through the muck only to die looked like the masts of shipwrecks. And perhaps some of them were. The history of all but the marsh was known. Nobody in the neighborhood was permitted to know more, or worse, to venture beyond the fence, and nobody had ever tried. At least, that was the official story. Liam had heard whispers about foolish souls who had braved the marsh, their inevitable demise accompanied by the sound of something immense and soggy shifting itself to accommodate the induction of more life to be processed into nutrients. Others said that a contributing factor to the death and decay of this part of the city had been the derailment of a train ferrying toxic materials, which Liam supposed might explain the presence of a marsh within the confines of a city, the strange fog, and the things rumored to live in its depths.

All Liam knew was that it smelled like wet dog and saltwater.

Against the wall stood a row of scarecrows, or rather the remains of them. On the Day of Leaves, these creatures had their burlap chests stuffed with dead vegetation before they were set alight. Now all that remained were the charred crosses and twisted shreds of material that called to mind the burnt bacon and eggs on his mother's stove. The scarecrow's hoods, though blackened by the flames, retained their shape. The sheep skulls that had been placed inside those hoods would be there for always. Only the straw bodies would be replaced.

And at the north end of the neighborhood, a twelve-foot wall of dead, twisted trees and vines at its back like some kind of cape, sat the church, watching him with stained glass eyes. The longer he stared, the more it seemed to tip its steepled hat at him, as if in acknowledgment. Lights flickered within as the last lingering penitents made their way through the aisles.

Without transition, it grew dark in an instant, long shadows yawning toward him from the open maw of the church.

Liam quickly averted his gaze and battled his way through the drifts to the pub.

* * *

There were half a dozen men inside, all of them clustered around the bar, all of them hunched over pints of whatever heady brown slop passed as ale. They fell silent as he entered, as if whatever they'd been discussing before his arrival was something not meant for his ears. He recognized them all as his neighbors, but if they recognized him in turn, it didn't show. All he saw were wary deep-set eyes over pale faces and stained beards. A fire crackled in a large open hearth in the corner, but the heat was occluded by a trio of men who were watching their shadows dance upon the wall.

McMahon's head rose like a gray egg above the cluster of men at the bar. His face was a mass of lines, his eyes like black pebbles in a stream. Tattoos of mermaids crawled up both arms as he braced them on the mahogany bar and scowled. "This is no place for you."

Feeling as if the attention of the whole room was on him, though only McMahon was looking at him directly, Liam swallowed and cast a hurried glance around at the men, hoping he might locate his father among them and therefore avoid having to engage McMahon in conversation. But his father wasn't here.

"I'm looking for—"

"I know who you're looking for. He'll be home when he's ready, and you can tell your mother that too. Haven't you learned your lesson by now?"

Again, Liam looked around. Clearly his father was here, somewhere, but he had already scanned the faces, or, when not made available for his study, the coats, and had come up empty. Where, then, was he? He put this question to McMahon, whose ruddy face seemed to darken with every second measured by the raven-faced clock above the bar.

"I told you to go home," he snapped. "And you'd better do it before you cause us any more trouble."

Liam stood immobile, helpless. If he returned home without his father, his mother would beat him to within an inch of his life. If he stayed, there was every chance McMahon would do the same. So, he said the only thing he could think of to buy him some time.

"I need to use the bathroom."

"Go outside in the snow," said McMahon.

Then, rather unexpectedly, a voice piped up from beneath the smoky glow of the amber lamps. Liam thought he recognized it as that of Mr. Wyman, his maritime studies teacher, but couldn't be sure because Wyman's voice tended to change depending on the weather.

"Let him look. None of this is our business anyway."

Though visibly displeased, McMahon threw up his hands and went back to scrubbing mildew from the beer taps. "As you like," he grumbled. "But it won't be on me. You can explain it to them when it all goes to hell."

Wyman—if that was indeed who had spoken from beneath the shelter of his tattered tweed jacket—breathed laughter that sounded like the snow huffing beneath the door. "We're all headed there anyway, McMahon. Doesn't matter in what order it takes us."

On the wall directly opposite where Liam stood was a cupboard with a missing door, inside which he could see an old dartboard. There were no numbers on the board, only symbols made of wire, symbols he recognized from his schoolbooks and the placard set into the stone block by the church door. The darts were made of boiled leather wrapped around shards of sharpened rat bones. Next to the board was a half rotted oak door that looked as if it had been designed for dwarves, but Liam knew it only appeared that way because time had forced it, like the rest of the building, to sink so that one had to step down into the adjacent room.

Eager to be free of the atmosphere his presence seemed to have generated among the gathering, Liam hurried to the door, grabbed the metal ring and shoved. Too large for its frame, the door resisted, the wood scraping against the stone lintel, the resultant sound monstrously loud in the confines of the small bar. Even the shadows seemed to shrink away from it. And then he was inside and forcing the door shut behind him.

He found himself in a narrow room with no windows and a ceiling so low he could touch it without fully extending his arm. Chaotic explosions of fungus gave the impression that the walls and ceiling were cushioned, or had been painted black, red, and gray. Broken chairs and tables had been stacked to the ceiling and back to the far wall so that there was little room to move. Liam had to skirt around them to reach the door in the far wall. When he did, he stopped, one hand on the ring, his heart in his throat.

Going beyond this point meant reliving his previous nightmare. The door led outside to an open-air bathroom covered only by a faltering tin roof, beneath which a single ceramic trough served as the place for men to relieve themselves. There were no facilities for women, because women never came here. There were no stalls. It was little more than a back alley with access blocked from the street by an avalanche of empty gas canisters and pulverized furniture.

Liam considered opening the door just a crack and calling his father's name, but he knew the howl of the wind and snow would likely make it inaudible. He lingered on the threshold, heart ramming against his ribs, until yet another voice entered the fray, this one more comforting than any other: *You can undo it. It will hurt at first like it always does, but you can take the pain. Later, when you're all alone, you can revise it and make it yours.* He had come to think of this soothing voice as echoes of his adult self, sent back through the mildewing pathways in his brain from some incomprehensible future, or a dream of one. And thus far, it had always steered him right.

Bracing himself, he yanked open the door and immediately recoiled at the stench of piss the snow blasted into his face. Grimacing, he wiped his nose on his glove and stepped out into the alley.

The single naked bulb suspended from the tin roof threw little light. The cobblestones out here were greasy and uneven and missing in places. With the warmth of the bar shut behind him, Liam wrapped his coat tighter around himself and squinted into the poor light. The trough where men did their business was empty of all but stains, discarded cigarette butts, and a half-inch of dark brown water, which bubbled and gurgled as if alive. Liam avoided looking too long at it as he made his way past the "toilet" and out into the area of yard unprotected by the sagging roof.

The snow buffeted his face like gravel as he surveyed the dark expanse before him. He stood still for a moment beside the calamity of gas cans and furniture blocking the exit until he detected a sound to his right, from the area next to the old tin shed where the darkness was thickest.

Last time he'd come here on such a mission, he had not needed to venture so far into the yard. On that occasion, he'd found his father sitting in the trough, pants around his ankles, face raised to the tin roof in ecstasy as the violin woman worked on him.

Yes, no women came to McMahon's Bar, but these visitors had been women in shape only. Nothing else about them suggested femininity. Nothing about them was remotely human. And of course, there wouldn't be. The church had sent them.

Liam dreaded coming upon such a scene again. It had taken him the better part of six months to recover from the last time, and only then because he had drawn sanity back into his head through his pictures. He knew he could do the same thing again now, no matter what he found, but he didn't want to have to experience it again first.

Unbidden, a small pulse of anger warmed the base of his throat and he frowned. Why had his mother made him come here again, knowing what he was likely to find? The answer, when it found him, was startling in its simplicity: they *wanted* him to see, *wanted* him to be driven mad, maybe in the hope that this time, it would take, and they'd finally be rid of him.

Incensed now, the anger spreading downward, setting fires throughout his chest and down into the pit of his stomach, he forgot his fear and made his way over to that suffocating swatch of darkness beside the old tin shed in which McMahon kept the spare barrels of beer, the moonshine, and the mason jars full of animals he had never had the heart to let go.

The sounds were louder here. Sounds he recognized despite being too young to know them. He stood there for some indeterminate amount of time until his eyes adjusted to the gloom and he could see the shapes, the nakedness, hear the passion as his father had his way with another one of *them*.

The violin lady was suspended above her father via her broken, twisted arms, her long-fingered hands clamped to the roof of the shed on one side, the wall on the other. She had no legs to speak of. Instead, her ragged torso ended in violin strings that started somewhere in her throat. Made taut by the concrete block suspended at the other end of the strings where the rest of her body should have been, the wind played a haunting tune she controlled by moving her mouth and working her throat. His father knelt before her, her bare breasts clamped in his dirty hands, his mouth working feverishly over her erect nipples. When she moaned, it was music; when he gasped, it was an ugly, hungry, desperate sound. His manhood was erect, stabbing pitifully at the empty air beneath the concrete block as she weaved from side to side.

The woman became aware of Liam first. She did not panic—they never did—instead she released one hand and then the other and dropped down into the darkness of the rubble until she was out of sight, the faint twanging of the violin strings the only indication that she was still there, hidden, as she alerted his father to their visitor.

The old man still had his hands before his face where the violin woman's breasts had been only a moment before. Slowly, as if surfacing from a dream, he dropped them and looked dazedly at the boy standing before him. The confusion quickly turned to rage as he rose like a wraith, tugging up his pants as he readied a hand to strike the boy.

"I fucking *told* you, I told *her* not to bother me," he said, a string of drool dangling from his lower lip. Even in the gloom, Liam could see the red glare in his eyes. He was drunk on more than just the beer.

Liam braced himself for the blow, his head turned slightly to the side, eyes shut tight.

It didn't come.

When next he opened his eyes, his father was staring uncertainly at him, something like fear on his long haggard face, both shivering from the cold.

"I'm allowed to do whatever I want here," his father said. "That's how it is now."

Discordant music as the violin woman skittered away down through a rent in the rubble. The old man looked over his shoulder with something like sadness before turning his attention back to his son. "I'm not coming home. I don't belong there anymore. But you know that already."

The snow whipped itself into a frenzy around them.

"I'll stay here and die with the rest of them. That's what was going to happen anyway. We all knew it. We just didn't expect it so soon. The gods can have us. I'm sure they won't turn us away. But whatever happens, this place can't last forever. Not like this. The city is dead."

Despite the anger, Liam shared his father's sadness. It didn't have to be this way. *Revise*, advised the voice he kept secret inside him, but he knew even if he did it would do nothing to erase the horror that lived on this side of things. All was darkness here, because it belonged here, and if it didn't stay contained in places such as these, it would corrupt everything.

"I'll go then," Liam said. "What should I tell Mother?"

His father shrugged on his coat, tied up his shirt and looked grimly at his son. "Whatever you want. It hardly matters now. She's lost, I'm lost. So are you." Then he walked by his son and went back inside the bar.

After a few moments of staring at the rubble and the life that was no longer hiding within the shadows, Liam turned and followed.

When he went inside, the crowd of men had doubled. Everyone in the neighborhood seemed to be there, except for the women, of course, all of whom would be at home tending to their sons and waiting for the end.

* * *

His mother was still standing by the stove when he returned with the bad news, but when she failed to answer him, he realized the blackening of the bacon and eggs had spread up to her elbows.

"I tried," he told her through the tears. "I always try. Sometimes it's just bigger than me and I can't make it any better."

She turned to look at him and he saw the grease sizzling in her eye sockets. Her hair fell out in clumps and landed in the frying pan, where it shriveled and died. When she opened her mouth to respond, he saw that it was full of straw, and as he looked on, the tears coming freely now, she collapsed in a heap on the floor. A sheep skull skittered across the stone and bumped against the leg of his chair, making it shriek.

Despondent at his failure, he went upstairs to his sanctuary and shut the door behind him.

Then he withdrew his sketchpad from beneath the bed.

His limited talents, which would not reach their full potential for years yet, perhaps ever, frustrated him as he erased and replaced and scratched and scribbled, but never got it right.

* * *

"Mr. Thompson, did you hear a word I said?"

Groggily, Liam raised his head from the protective darkness of his arms. When the other children saw that he'd been sleeping, a fine thread of drool connecting his lips to his desk, they giggled nervously. Nobody would outright laugh at him. They knew his history, knew what he'd done, and that only the fact that he was so young had kept him from being stuck in a white room with rubber walls somewhere.

Blinking away the confusion, Liam looked up at his teacher. Dressed bat-like in the professorial robes typical of teachers in Catholic boys' schools, Mr. Wyman clucked his tongue and grabbed the sketchpad from the desk. "More of this macabre doodling? Mr. Thompson, I daresay if you put half as much effort into your language studies as you did these...these..." He gestured helplessly at the peculiar, morbid rendition of their church and the school and the myriad monsters his subconscious suggested could inhabit them and tossed the pad aside. It hit the desk with bang.

"Focus, child," the teacher said, and headed back to the top of the class.

Bright autumn sunshine turned the windows to gold and flooded the room with light, illuminating the dust. At Wyman's request, the other children gradually tore their attention away from Liam, from the weird kid, and returned their attention to the scrawl of French on the chalkboard.

"Je m'appelle *John*," Wyman instructed, his patrician smile aimed at every child in turn as he punctuated the air with a wizened finger as if it were a conductor's baton. "Je m'appelle *Rebecca*."

Liam tried to return his focus to the classroom, to the fraudulent construct his mind had created to protect himself from the wrath of the gods. Even though Wyman had moved away and let him be, he knew there would be consequences. Lately he was falling asleep more often, found it almost impossible to concentrate. His grades were dropping and the few friends who didn't hold his past against him had drifted away. He was stared at in the halls, mocked in gym, bullied in the bathroom. And then home, the most dreaded place of all, where his mother did her best to make it seem as if the divorce was not tearing her asunder. She too had quit the pretense of being a loving mother, confining him to his room with his books and his drawings. Sometimes late at night he could hear her weeping through the wall. Sometimes early in the morning he heard her talking on the phone and screaming about her "loser husband" and that "musician whore he shacked up with."

None of it meant anything to Liam. He was safe in his sanctuary where everything was under his control. He could exist between these two worlds, but not forever. Sooner or later he would have to find a way to tie them together so some kind of balance could be restored.

He glanced out the window through the glorious fraudulent day and saw the church on the horizon. Pristine, uncorrupted, normal. Dead leaves fell silently through the amber haze as the trees began to reveal their true selves. The city was like a held breath. Soon it would be time again to fill the scarecrows.

"Mr. Thompson?"

He snapped to attention and looked at Mr. Wyman, with his sweeping gray hair and rosy cheeks. "Yes, sir?"

"Eyes up here, please."

"Yes, sir."

"Comment tu t'appelles?"

"Je m'appelle Liam."

"Très bon." He began to pace, his focus moving to another child. "Alex? Comment t'allez vouz?"

Liam went back to pretending, but not before checking the ceiling behind him where in the corner nearest the door, the mold was starting to spread.

A WICKED THIRST

I WAKE UP DROWNING IN A PUDDLE, my lungs filled with rainwater. Through the panic, only one thought is clear: *I am going to die.* This stark certainty is enhanced to a horrible degree when I attempt to raise my head and find resistance, something pushing back against my skull, keeping all but my eyes submerged. Someone is trying to kill me. In this moment, perhaps one of the few I have left, the nature of my enemy is irrelevant. It matters only that he is there standing over me, his boot against the back of my head pressing down, down, down, and that he will not relent until the life or the fight has left me.

* * *

"You like to drink, huh?"

Melinda says it with no accusation in her voice. If anything, she looks amused, and that's good. Too many of these dates have been wrecked by judgment.

Over my glass of bourbon, I shrug and offer her what you might call a "wry smile", though I only employ it to avoid opening my mouth and letting the world see my teeth. The few remaining people in my life who still call themselves friends claim this doesn't matter, that anyone who cares enough about me would be willing to disregard this aesthetic flaw. But I know this world. I see the celebrities beaming their pristine, expensive smiles at us mere mortals, and I've thwarted many an incumbent lover by admitting upfront that my dental state is not pretty. Even long-term lovers (back when long-term was a logical assumption) used it as ammunition during arguments because they know I'm self-conscious about it. They know it hurts, so it's an easy play. *You're a waste of space, a goddamn drunk, and don't get me started on those fucking teeth. Ugh!* I want to say that if I had the money, I'd get them fixed, but that's not true. I've had the money plenty of times, and it was then, as it is now, much easier to drink away the need to care. That the alcohol and the cigarettes are what destroyed my teeth in the first place is a truth that doesn't hinder me at all.

"Sure, who doesn't?" I say, in response to Melinda's question. She plays with the swizzle stick in her own drink, a cocktail of some indeterminate origin. The glass is enormous and rimed with sugar, the liquid within the color of a sunrise. I've never understood pretty drinks. Lethality should come in a more obvious costume, don't you think? The amount of alcohol in that rowboat-sized receptacle reinforces the hope that no lecture about abstinence is forthcoming, so I allow myself to relax a little.

"My parents," she tells me, with a sigh, and to this I can relate.

"Yours too, huh. Religious?"

"Catholic."

"Same."

"To the lapsed."

We raise our glasses and toast gently, with no real celebration, because the ugliness of the truth we just shared is something that deserves only to be buried, not commemorated. Then again, who I am these days is commemoration enough of that dark time in my life.

We're seated at a moderately well-lit booth in a bar-restaurant hybrid, better known these days as a *gastropub*, a name which never fails to make me think of beer farts. This whole area of town is trying hard to be upscale and failing gradually. If the demand isn't there, it doesn't matter how glossy your business looks or how high you hike the real estate prices. Now when you walk this neighborhood, it's not difficult to imagine what the big glass and brass frontages will look like with shutters.

At the bar, a line of businessmen and women flirt and talk shop much too loudly while spending too much money. Around them, as attendant as bees, harried looking waiters and bar staff with no money at all rush around them trying not to look miserable and annoyed. All of them are slightly blurred, and not only because my focus is directed at Melinda, but also because it's been a long day, and I've marked three quarters of the hours I've been awake with either a cheap beer or a midrange bourbon.

I'm spending money I don't have. Child support money I tell myself I can make back before it summons trouble. Sometimes this is even true.

"Am I losing you already?" Melinda asks, and despite the permanent fixture of her amused smile, I suspect it won't be long before the phone comes out and she gets a "surprise" text and with it, the apology that she must get going to attend to some sudden and unavoidable event.

"No," I tell her, and wonder if the dimming of the lights is actual or imagined. "Rough day, and I'm finding myself seduced by the ambience and the company."

Her smile widens just enough to let me know she appreciates the compliment but recognizes its fragility. "Nothing at all to do with the three bourbons you've sunk since we sat down?"

Her math is wrong. I've been taking hits from my pocket flask in the men's room. Part of it is whatever compels me to never get close enough to sobriety to feel the real tragedy of my existence. I know how pitiful that sounds, but it doesn't change the reality of it. Another part of it is nerves, because the simple truth is this: I've had a lot of women. This is not a boast, just a fact. I'd make a list if I could recall half of them, but I can't, so you'll just have to take my word that we're probably talking close to a hundred. Without drink, that number would be less than ten, because I've never known how to talk to women—or anyone else for that matter—unless I'm buzzed. Walk in on me in a bar halfway through the night and you'd think I was perfectly at ease, comfortable in my skin, and just the best damn company. Charming, if a little quiet, confident but not cocky, and you'd be right. Catch me in the morning and you'll end up calling the suicide hotline on my behalf. Catch me in the company of women before I've had a shot and I look like a man afraid to address his own reflection. I don't like that person. Truth to tell, I don't much like either of them, but at least there's something I can do about the lesser one. That confidence with women, forced or not, worked better back in the day, before my looks began to fade. That Melinda is sitting across from me now is nothing short of a miracle, though on such occasions I figure my idea of a miracle is closer to pity than I'd like to admit.

"Do you do this often?" she asks, waving a hand between us.

"Dating?"

She nods.

"On and off for the past year. Mostly off."

"Only a year?"

"Considered trying it earlier but marriage got in the way."

"Ah."

"Yeah. Soon as the divorce hit, I signed right up to see what I'd been missing."

"And did it meet your expectations?"

"Not until tonight."

She rolls her eyes and sits back. She doesn't blush or fawn. I can see she appreciates the compliment. I can also see it's a line she's heard a lot and which, consequently, has lost all value. Her green-eyed gaze is penetrating, as if she's been asking me the real important questions all night long without ever opening her mouth. Her hair is long, dark, and wavy, her bare shoulders sprinkled with freckles. I like her. I think the sober me would adore her, but that's a question destined to remain unanswered, not because I don't plan to see her if all goes well, but because I'm unlikely to be sober when and if I do.

She sits forward again, takes a short sip from her cocktail and crosses her arms on the table. "So, tell me, what's been your worst date so far?"

I scrunch up my face, and then remember the expression exposes my teeth, and switch instead to studious pondering, a forefinger to my lips to seal them. "Hmm."

"Want me to go first?"

I nod, and she does.

"I won't bore you with prefaces or qualifiers or buildup. I'll just get straight to it. First off, the guy looked nothing like his profile picture, which is always the dread expectation."

I resist the urge to interject that she doesn't either. She looks better. But I'm already pushing my luck in the flattery regard, so I do what all good men are supposed to do, and just listen. It's not easy though. As people are fond of telling me, one of the characteristics that emerge when I'm drinking is an inability to shut the fuck up, and I feel that now, the urgent and omnipresent bubbling of words in my throat. It's almost like I sometimes think if I don't make a sound, I'm not really there, or that I'm in imminent danger of being forgotten if I'm not part of the conversation.

"He was older, had less hair, and was considerably fatter than he appeared in his picture. I admit to being disappointed, but I'm also not superficial, so I can deal with disappointment in the looks arena if the personality compensates. Is that crass?"

"Not at all," I tell her. "Unless you're classifying me the same way."

Another eyeroll. "Nooo. Anyway, with this guy, not only had he lied about his looks, he wasn't even interested in a date."

"Then why sign up for a dating site?"

"I know, right? Sometimes people baffle me."

"So, what was his deal?"

"Religious crusade."

"Christ."

"Exactly. He spent twenty minutes lecturing me on my vices, said only godless whores put themselves out there on a public site with the intention—his words—of forcing men to compromise their spiritual beliefs through sexual perversion."

I chuckle at this while noting my glass is somehow empty again. Without taking my eyes from Melinda, who is clearly enjoying recounting the story, I raise a hand to summon a waiter.

"So, what did you say?"

She shrugs. "Told him he was absolutely right, that had he not been good enough to call me out as a heathen, I'd have lured him home and let him do anything he wanted to me. Then I thanked him for saving me from myself and left him there with the check."

The waiter appears. It might as well be a mannequin for all the life that's in his eyes. I order another round and tell him to cheer up. His tight smile appears to be all that's holding back a torrent of abuse. I can't blame him. It's a shit job for shit pay made worse when customers like me offer unsolicited advice.

"The best part?" Melinda says, tears of mirth in her eyes. "There was absolutely no victory on his face when I told him he was right. He looked crestfallen, like he regretted not getting to see what I'd have let him do to me. Fucking hypocrites, hiding behind judgment of others to protect themselves from their own impulses." She grabs a napkin and delicately dabs the moisture from her eyes without ruining her makeup. "Who the fuck goes out on dates just to preach?"

"Amen, sister."

"Okay, your turn."

"Mine's weird."

"Oh goody. Tell me."

"I'll spare you the worst of it. The short version is I met a woman who looked like a supermodel. Thought I'd won the lottery because unlike *your* guy she showed up looking exactly like her profile picture."

"Did she have a dick?"

"No, that I could have handled. Excuse the pun."

Melinda snorts laughter. That and the slight glassy look in her eyes tells me the alcohol is settling in, and that's good. I work better when people are, if not on my level, then at least in the same building.

"We have dinner, we connect. It all goes great. We end up back at her place."

"Just like that, huh? Floozy."

"I guess the chemistry was just there."

"Uh-huh."

"Fiery."

"Right."

"Sooo...we get there, beautiful house, nice cars parked out front and I'm thinking she comes from money. It's starting to look like I've hit the jackpot..."

"And...what?"

"And we get inside, and her parents are waiting for us."

"Oh, no." She raises her eyebrows, puts a hand over her mouth.

"I'm thinking: shit, she's younger than she looked and now I'm in Dutch. But that wasn't it. Her parents were just really nice, open, understanding people. They invited me in, and we all sat down for drinks. The father, real congenial sort, tells me about his fiscal year at the law firm. The mother, a little drunk, throws flirty eyes at me and quizzes me on my background. And then, when the conversation ebbs, they apologize for getting in the way and leave us to, as the father put it: 'Consummate our night.'"

"Oh God, and...did you?"

"Are you kidding me? The cab couldn't get there fast enough."

"Wow."

"Yeah, but the worst part is she stalked me for like a month. I had to delete my Facebook page." I raise my hand to grab the waiter's attention again. He looks at me somewhat witheringly. "Then her father started calling and leaving me voicemails, apologizing for scaring me off and asking if I'd give his daughter another chance."

Melinda loses it, her laugh so loud everyone at the bar looks in our direction.

* * *

Somehow, I manage to turn my head so that half my face is out of the water, but only for a moment. I have time to see the shadowy shapes of darkened houses backlit by the sickly glow of streetlights before the pressure returns and slams my face back down into the muddy water.

And those teeth, such a source of shame for so long, shatter against the asphalt.

* * *

"This is the weird part," Melinda says.

"Like the rest of the night hasn't been?"

She stops on the pavement outside the restaurant and appraises me with as much seriousness as her condition will allow. She's weaving slightly on her feet, one hand clamped on my shoulder for support, which, given my own state, is like leaning two ladders against each other on an ice rink. "Is that criticism? Did it go bad? Badly? Whatever it is?"

I feel a swell of affection for her, and it's far from the first. She's beautiful: curvy, smart, bubbly, funny, she's everything a guy could want. And most importantly, she drinks. And while I can handle people who don't, I prefer that they do. Sober people see straight through me much too quickly.

"I think it went great. And I think you're amazing."

Now that the alcohol has softened her filter, she blushes and draws close. I can smell the strawberry vodka on her breath, and it's wonderful. Her eyes are like shot glasses full of crème du menthe. Her smile is uneven, uncertain, and tinged with mischief. "I don't date alcoholics."

A shrug. "Me neither."

She snorts laughter again and appraises me as if for the first time. The people on the street around us become a blur. "*I'm* not an alcoholic."

I believe this to be true. "But you're an addict."

She considers this, staggers a little and puts her free hand on my other shoulder for support. It looks like we're about to dance. "I've been too fond of many things in my lifetime: booze, painkillers, pot, but the only thing I've ever really developed an incurable and destructive addiction to is men. Pricks like you who come along out of nowhere to make me feel good about myself for a while, even if it's all just so much bullshit in the end, and even if the effect is only ever temporary and leaves me feeling even more empty and depressed afterward."

I don't protest her classification of me, because I don't know that she's wrong. I'd love to purport to have noble motives in this instance, but really it would all be so much self-delusion and deception. I'm here with her because I'm lonely. I need someone to talk to, to drink with, and, all going well, to sleep with. If I could choose only one option, it would be the second one, because ultimately that's the only constant, the only requirement my soul needs when the darkness is at its worst. The only real need. But even so, loneliness can, like everything else, be drowned. The date was just a feeble attempt to make it look to myself like I'm trying to rebuild a normal life, and yet I contacted Melinda because I knew from her profile that she wasn't ready for that. Something about the forced confidence in her sales pitch. Even if she decided to take the chance, she certainly wasn't ready for me and my unruly shadow.

Maybe I was wrong and she's not an addict, at least not in any traditional sense, but she's here with me because she needs something she's not getting, and it's more than just sex or the casual company of another. Perhaps it's nothing more complicated than validation, the very ordinary need to be appreciated, but isn't that an addiction, too?

"Come back to me," she says, and follows it with the same sound one makes when trying to summon a cat. "Did I blow it?"

I offer her a sly smile. "No."

"Good."

"But you can if you want to."

"Jesus, is that a line that ever actually works?"

"Not really," I tell her and join her in laughing.

But this time, it does.

* * *

I don't know how I ended up here, shivering from the cold, wearing nothing but my boxers as someone tries to drown me in a brackish puddle. I can taste the rainwater, the blood, the grainy pieces of my broken teeth on my tongue. My thoughts spin in a mad vortex of self-preservation.

Finally, the pressure relents. I roll over on my back, sobbing from the pain, the humiliation, the confusion, and see the dark figure looming over me. He is backlit by the streetlights, which makes his face a mystery, but I know who he is, and dread squeezes my heart so tightly I fear it may stop.

"Please...don't," I beg him.

"Get up," he says.

I start to sob and bring my hands to my face to cover my eyes.

I pray I'm dreaming, and know that I'm not.

He found me again.

* * *

Time has a way of contracting when you're drinking. I met Melinda at eight, and by midnight we're back at her place, but it feels like an hour has passed between us. Her house is small but spotless aside from a few dishes in the sink and a scattering of dry cat food around a bowl on the kitchen floor. The cat itself is nowhere to be seen, and for this I'm grateful. I used to be a cat person until my daughter's tabby was mauled by the neighbor's dog and I had to put it out of its misery. Sitting beside the small mound of dirt in the backyard that night, I drank myself into a stupor and cried, not for the cat, not even for my daughter, but for memories of things that had happened to me as a child, things I had buried deeper than poor Chuckles the cat and were thus much harder to exhume. But I felt them, mourned the loss of who I might have been, and when my wife, eyes narrowed by sleep, came out to check on me, I attacked her for reasons unknown.

That was the only time she had to call the cops on me, and because incarceration came to mean sobriety, and a terrifying, disorientating, nightmarish kind of hangover, just the threat of it kept me in line for the future. If you've ever gone out for a few beers and woken up startled to find yourself in a jail cell surrounded by mad, violent, and similarly confused people, you know what I mean. I had no desire to go back. That's when I learned the trick to secret drinking and the benefits of false sobriety.

"You're a deep one," Melinda says, pulling me back out of myself for the umpteenth time since we met. We're sitting on her comfy sofa before a dark TV, close enough that our knees are touching. Before me, on the low glass and mahogany coffee table, is a glass of white wine. I'm not a big fan of wine. It tends to make me nauseous if I mix it with bourbon, but that won't keep me from drinking it. Right now, wine is as good a poison as anything else.

"I'm out of practice," I explain with a sheepish look. "I've forgotten how much fun this can be, and I think I'm being distant out of some silly fear that I'll do or say the wrong thing, y'know?"

God, if she only knew.

Since returning from the bathroom, she has touched up her hair and makeup and taken drops to remove the redness from her eyes. She looks as good as she has all night. I wonder how I look and dismiss the question almost immediately. It will do me no favors to ponder it.

"Just relax and be yourself. You've managed to lure me back to my place and thus far I haven't screamed or called the police. You've scored. Chill." Grinning, she raises her glass. I grab mine and we toast.

Looking into her eyes, I feel a transient calm. I'm happy to be here, with her. There's no future in it and I think we both know that. But for the moment I feel, dare I say it, human. Normal.

Safe.

* * *

He grabs me by the hair and lifts me bodily off the street until I'm forced to stand. My legs are shaking from the cold and the terror. I silently will someone, anyone in that darkened row of houses behind us to wake and come out to see what the commotion is, to call the police, to run to my aid, something, anything. The houses have nothing to say.

But I know, deep inside where the truth hides, that even if someone did come to my aid, it would do no good.

"This is a dream," I manage to gasp, and my attacker responds by driving a fist into my stomach. It feels like he is wearing a glove made of concrete. My knees buckle, and I blurt vomit onto my feet, but I can't fall because now he has me by the throat.

"I could kill you," he says, and I know he's telling the truth, because once upon a time he tried to save me, and it killed him instead.

* * *

I am lying naked on her bed, stripes of shadow across my chest from the light through her bedroom blinds. I have one hand behind my head, the other in her hair as she attends to me. My eyes are closed, and I am wincing, not from desire but embarrassment, because in my mind I am hard as a rock, a shockingly becocked paragon of virility, but in reality, she has been trying to evoke a reaction from that treacherously flaccid member for what seems like forever. If I possessed any residue of male pride, I would claim, if only to myself, that this was an aberration, but it isn't. Sometimes I'm lucky and whatever blend of alcohol I have imbibed on a given night quite literally throws me a bone, but more often than not, I'm left dead from the waist down despite the will to perform. It is an eventuality I frequently forget. Eventually, she gives up and I await her judgment. But when her face resolves from the dark, she is smiling, my useless cock lying dead in the shadowed valley between her pendulous breasts.

"I'm sorry," I tell her. "I guess I had one too many."

She kisses her way up my chest to my neck and then rolls over on her back beside me. "It happens," she says, and spreads her legs, knees drawn up. "Maybe *you'll* have better luck."

Relieved that my failure to rise to the occasion has not killed the moment or become something to be taken as a personal affront to her sex appeal, I shimmy down and kneel at the end of the bed. The smell of her sex is almost as intoxicating as the finest bourbon. Her fingers find my hair and force my lips to hers. I slide my tongue inside her. I drink deep of the salty sweet taste as she bucks against me, moaning low in her throat. My hands knead her buttocks, pulling her tighter against my mouth. I miss the intimacy, the closeness, the warmth, and the sheer *giving* involved in such acts. It is one of the few things I can offer anymore. When Melinda comes, she throws her head back against the pillow, mouth wide, hands flying up to grab the rails of the headboard. Her body shudders once, twice, and again, and she utters a single staggered "Ohhhh," and grows still. I am aware that as aroused as she makes me in my head and my soul, my cock still refuses to obey.

Thankfully, it doesn't appear to be an issue.

"Cuddle with me, loverboy." With a contented smile on her face, Melinda reaches for me. I climb atop her, my face buried in those voluminous breasts with their incongruently tiny nipples, and within minutes, we are both asleep.

But my mouth tastes like salt, and I am thirsty.

So thirsty now.

* * *

I am struggling in vain to be free of him as he carries me back toward the house I now realize is Melinda's. His hand around my throat is like a tourniquet keeping the scream from bleeding free. I try to kick him and it is like kicking a brick wall. Any moment now I might die. I am already seeing stars.

But how did I get from the bed to the street outside?

"Blackout, you fucking loser," he tells me, his voice like someone rattling bottlecaps in a wool pocket. "You woke, you walked, and you ended up in the middle of the street with your dick out, trying to take a piss."

I want to think he's wrong, but I know he isn't. In life, he never misled me. In death, there's even less of a motive to lie. And it's not like this isn't a regular event. Most nights I can't remember how I ended up wherever I find myself, and the panic and confusion debilitates me.

I can move only my eyes, and I see the small wrought iron gate leading to the driveway of Melinda's house. Her car comes into view, then fills my vision entirely as my face is slammed into the side of it, a move which has the instantaneous effect of setting off the alarm. It screeches and squawks into the night as I am thrown against it, an alcoholic wretch in his underwear covered in rain and blood and gasping for air.

A few moments later the front door flies open and through rapidly swelling eyes, I see Melinda standing there, hair tousled, tugging a robe closed to hide her nakedness, her face jaundiced by the flashes of amber light from her car.

"What the *fuck?*" she asks and disappears back inside the house. A second later, long enough for me to see that my attacker has vanished, she reappears, points her keys at the car and hits a button. The car shrieks once more and falls silent.

"I'm sorry. I'm sorry, Abby. I was thirsty. I got lost. I'm sorry."

"Abby?" Melinda says, but she doesn't look annoyed, merely concerned. I've seen that look too many times before to trust in it. It never lasts. Instead it mutates over time into frustration, hatred and resentment. Most people are not equipped to deal with my problems. People like me. People like my ex-wife Abby, or my poor kids. Or Melinda.

Why am I here?

What the fuck was I thinking?

Certainly not about the cat, the cutest cat you ever did see, who I killed with the shovel to end his pain.

Certainly not my friends, none of whom will answer the phone.

Certainly not about my sponsor, who is dead, and won't leave me alone.

"I'm sorry," I say again, and then I am weeping openly, hopelessly into my hands. The cuts on my face and mouth sting, sobering me, bringing me, however temporarily, back to the wasteland I have made for myself. My gums ache as if someone has tied strings around them and is trying to pull them down my throat.

A soft touch. An arm around my shoulders. A body seated next to me on the cold ground, in the rain, pressing against me. Fingers stroking my hair, a cheek pressed against the top of my head. Comfort.

My God, how I wish so desperately I could escape into love, into her, and hide inside her warmth forever. But I am my own anchor, and it always pulls me back into the cold reality of a world with no solid edges save one: the bottom.

"I'm sorry. I don't know what's wrong with me."

"It's okay," Melinda says. I wonder why that's so. What has happened to *her*? What other monsters has she endured to bring her to a place where a broken wretch like me is okay under *any* circumstances?

I raise my head and she looks at me, those eyes green even in the dark. Her mouth is a tight line of worry. "Why don't you come back inside and get cleaned up? I can make us some coffee."

"Is there any wine left?" I ask, as panic begins to weave outward from its spindle at the center of my chest. I won't look, but I can see the man standing behind her now, a blockade between us and the open front door. The rain passes through him, but he is too real to be a ghost.

"I need a drink, Melinda," I tell her, because that's what the presence of that raging figure means. It's what it has always meant.

"I know, but I'm not sure that's such a good idea."

The figure, too tall, too thin, too disproportionate, moves closer without moving at all. Even in the light from the streetlamps, he has no features, and that is a mercy. But I remember what he looks like all too clearly. No amount of drink can erase that from my beleaguered mind.

"Please take me inside."

She does, helping me up as if I'm a ninety-year-old man with no flesh left on his bones. She leads me back inside the house and closes the door on the rain.

And on *him*.

* * *

She makes us coffee. While she's busy in the kitchen, I drain the last dregs of wine from the bottle we left on the coffee table, then from our wineglasses. I wish I'd left some for just this occasion, an occasion I should have known would come. Nowadays it nearly always does. I drink to forget what drinking has done and that only seems to make it worse, summoning specters I can never outrun.

Namely, the sponsor.

"You might need stitches," Melinda says, setting the coffee down before me. The smell of it activates my gag reflex. "And, my God, what happened to your teeth?"

I pull away from her attempt at an oral examination, no less ashamed of my teeth now despite the absence of three of the worst offenders.

"I need a drink." The desperation in my voice is terrifying.

"We finished it," she says. "And nothing's likely to be open at this hour."

"Something must be."

I have already searched my coat and found the flask empty. I can't remember when I finished it off, but that hardly matters now.

"I'm here for you," she says, and I know she means it. "Talk to me."

There are two kinds of concern, I've found. The first is closer to pity, with no commitment for the sympathizer to make any active effort to change the circumstances of the afflicted. It's a passing concern, you might say, and makes the observer feel better just for feeling it. And then there are people like Melinda, who are not repulsed by tragedy but perversely attracted to it, less out of any legitimate philanthropy and more because it makes them feel needed, necessary, a consequence of their own affliction: an inability to accurately gauge their own self-worth, which makes it directly proportionate to the well-being of another. Next to me is a beautiful woman who has and maybe never will believe that she is a wonderful person because she will spend her life courting people and situations designed to hurt her. It explains her patience, the look of recognition and lack of alarm when she found me outside. She has seen, if not this, then something comparable before. Maybe even something worse. But she doesn't quite yet know how bad this is.

"Please find me something. Nail polish remover. Cleaning fluid. I don't care. I just...I can't be sober. Not right now. Not for a while. Please." I'm aware that I sound like a child, but I can't afford to care. I feel hollow inside, dangerously close to exploding into panic and who knows what else if I don't pacify the demon.

"Just calm down," she says, moving closer.

I look at her and wince at a bolt of pain. This one is not from my injuries, but from my liver and kidneys, where it feels as if my shadowy attacker has buried his hands in me.

"Are you all right?" Her warm hand on the nape of my neck is like the hand of God.

"No. No I'm not. The sponsor found me."

"The what?"

"The man I killed."

I feel her stiffen, but she doesn't yet move away. "Tell me," she says.

"I will, but please, find me something to drink."

At first, she resists, but as I sit there dabbing the blood from my ruptured gums, my eyes full of tears, I see the pity take over and, with a shake of her head, she begins a cursory search of the house. It doesn't take long before she returns with a bottle of rubbing alcohol.

"Tell me," she says again, "And after that, I'm taking you to the hospital."

I do not argue.

"And you need to sip. Small sips or it'll kill you."

Ignoring her, I take a gulp from the bottle. It's hell on my wounds, burns its way like molten lava down my throat, and curdles in my stomach. But it works, if only to pacify the panic that courses through my veins like a living, lunatic thing. After exhaling the fumes on a noxious sigh, I tell Melinda about Stephen Carver.

* * *

The first time my wife threatened to leave me and take our kids away, I pacified her by promising to quit drinking. It was not an empty promise, or at least, not consciously empty. I was willing to try whatever it took to get better, so I stripped the house of alcohol, shocked as I did so by how many secret stashes I uncovered. It began to bring it home to me just how far gone I was. And yes, I'm aware how fucked up it sounds that after all the arguments and embarrassments, the violence and the arrest, it was the discovery of those bottles that delivered to me the message that all was not well.

So, out they went, and I altered my mental routine in an effort to stay dry.

I lasted three months before I dropped my phone while in bed and found the cheap plastic bottle of vodka stashed behind the nightstand. I left it there, waited for my wife to fall asleep, and then took the bottle down to the garage. There, in the dark, after a struggle I like to mischaracterize as titanic and torturous, when it was pretty brief and insincere, I drank the whole fucking thing. Though I'd anticipated it, there was no guilt, no shame, no disappointment in myself. Instead, I felt right, like I'd allowed myself to be me again. Things changed after that. I made some concessions for the sake of my marriage. I kept regular hours, drank at work instead of at bars, made sure I smelled good, and behaved like a good husband and father. I also took to staying awake and drinking in my garage.

Which is where Abby found me one night in late summer, choking on my own vomit.

Hospital. Stomach pump. Detox. AA.

I went to counseling, and even found a sponsor. He was an old grizzled guy, eighteen years dry, who liked to spout philosophies and share Buddhist wisdoms while sitting too close to me and touching me far too often. His teeth were too big, his eyes too small. His name was Stephen Carver and he *knew* what I was going through, *understood* it, had been there himself and *vowed* to be there and guide me through my darkest hours when I needed him. Only, I didn't want to get better, and ultimately that's what undid me then and undoes me still. I don't *want* to be better. I want to just ride this train in the safety of numbness until it goes right off the edge of a cliff and takes me with it. What I don't like and can't seem to stop from happening, is hurting other people along the way. People like my wife, who quit on me once she'd admitted me to the hospital, and my kids, who still don't really understand when and how and why I became a monster. People like you, Melinda, who try so very, very hard to be there and to heal me and to listen, when really there's nothing to say that's worth hearing. And people like Stephen Carver, a man I hated with a passion just for forcing me to be perpetually aware of my disease. And it is a disease. This, I know. It's a maddening thirst that never goes away and it cares little about the source as long as it, and I, am sustained.

Christmas Eve of last year. My first Christmas alone, without the kids. Abby allowed me to see them for an hour. I'd lost my job and could only afford to get them gifts from the dollar store, which they were too young to be able to fake appreciating. Abby stood in the corner, watching, making no attempt to hide her distaste for my apartment, which was admittedly a fleapit. On her face, I saw no regret, no love, no wishful thinking that things had worked out differently. I saw only condemnation and disgust and anger, all of which I deserved. The whole affair was awkward, and forced, and I knew when my kids left with Abby, I would never see them again.

That night I went out and bought a bottle of whiskey.

I drank half of it before I thought of calling my sponsor.

He was disappointed, obviously, and concerned, but also as good as his word. He promised to come see me and we'd talk. On Christmas Eve! What a guy!

But he never made it. The lowered blade of a fucking snowplow sideswiped his Toyota a mile and a half from my house. He spun the wheel and slammed into a streetlight. Went straight out through the windshield. He didn't die instantly. They hospitalized him. I got a call from Todd Nolan, the irritant who kept us all in line at our AA meetings and spoke to everyone like a priest. He filled me in, said he knew Stephen had been on his way to see me. Thought I should know Stephen was in the hospital. He gave me a breakdown of the injuries, but the gist of it was that he had hit the pole headfirst, shattered his neck and spine, blinded himself, ruptured his spleen, brain damage, internal bleeding....and so on and so forth. It wasn't looking good. He asked me to come see Stephen. I said I would. I didn't. Instead I shut myself up in the apartment and sat beside my pitiful wretch of a Christmas tree and drank myself into oblivion.

The next day the phone rang again and again and again. I ignored it but saw the text from Todd.

Stephen has passed.

And with it, all last lingering shreds of my sobriety.

The twist in the tale, the truly funny thing about it all, is that any guilt I might have felt or feel still is mitigated by something else Todd texted me, a week or so later.

Did you know Stephen had been drinking that night?

All his wisdom, all his promises, and the fucking guy was on the sauce, still. No wonder he was so secure in his pontificating. It was all bullshit. So, now I tell myself he shouldn't have been driving, and that he was on his way to share a drink with me, not berate me for lapsing, when he had the accident. I tell myself he swerved into the path of that snowplow, maybe because very secretly, behind that smarmy façade, he wanted to die. Just like I do.

He's dead, Melinda. Dead deep down in the drunken dirt.

And I saw him tonight. I see him almost every time I black out.

But when it's bad, when I'm truly lost, only then does he make me suffer.

* * *

I emerge from my bitter reverie and open my eyes. My throat is dry from talking and I am startled to find myself alone in the dark. I am still on the sofa, though I have switched sides. I'm sitting where Melinda sat only moments before, though I can't be sure it was moments and not hours. The scent of her fills my nose. Her perfume and a metallic, coppery smell. I am cold and shivering and there is something wet on my chest. I must have spilled the rubbing alcohol while I was telling my tale.

I need a drink.

"Melinda?"

I stand on shaky legs, bracing my hand on the arm of the couch for support and try to blink the room into focus. Sinister shapes hunched over in the dark reveal themselves to be nothing but the furniture.

"Where are you?"

Something soft brushes against my shin and I scream.

The cat bolts from me with a hiss, its claws skittering against the hardwood, and I stagger back against the wall, barely preventing a lamp from falling to the floor.

A few moments to catch my breath. *It's all right*, I counsel myself. *It's okay. You just fell asleep. Wandered. It's all right.*

The house is dead and dark.

Clumsily, unsteadily, I make my way to the stairs. Feel the agony of drink-starved limbs and organs tightening in protest and practically climb the steps on all fours. I so often awake consumed with dread and confusion and the stark certainty that everything is horribly wrong that more than once I have considered finding something sharp and cutting my throat before I am forced to confront whatever it is. My days have become a reel of badly edited scenes. Cut together, they make little sense. I am afraid to sleep, afraid to be awake. I don't even know if the people I meet are real anymore. I'm the product of some ill-advised experiment to monitor the body's reaction to obscene quantities of alcohol, to see the emotional cost and the time it takes to go insane.

Upstairs and the halls are drenched in shadow and moonlight. Gingerly, I navigate the chiaroscuro, afraid those crooked bars of darkness might snap shut and cut me into pieces. The floorboards creak beneath my feet. I hear the clicking of the cat's claws on the stairs behind me.

"Melinda?"

Her bedroom door, slightly ajar, is at the end of the hall. For a moment, it appears to move away from me, obviating my progress, as if in mockery. I will it to stand still. I need Melinda now as much as I have needed her all night and feel a pang of guilt that I have burdened her with this. I need her eyes, her warmth, her understanding and patience. I need her to be the anchor that keeps the tide from casting me back into the current just for a little while longer.

I open the door. It makes no sound.

The sponsor is standing in the corner. He lights a cigarette, it lights up his face, or rather, where his face used to be before the windshield glass sheared it away. His voice, when he speaks, is the sound of a rusty saw through a stubborn stump.

"Welcome back."

I look at the shape on the bed. Melinda is half-naked and lying on her back, the sheets covering her lower body. Both arms are by her sides. I approach, my heart beating so violently it is as if the sponsor is punching a rhythm into my back.

"What...what did you do to her?" I ask, and almost fall over on top of Melinda as my thighs meet the mattress.

Her skin is pale as alabaster, except where the blood has run and pooled. The sheets are dark beneath her.

"What did you do?" I scream at the shape in the corner.

He chuckles. "I did nothing."

My hands flutter over her body like butterflies. I want to touch. I'm afraid to touch, but I don't see any wounds and her hair is covering her face. Could the blood be mine?

"You were thirsty," the sponsor says, expelling blue smoke. "So, you drank."

I bend over and move Melinda's hair away from her face. Her mouth is slightly open. So are her eyes. I tap her cheek gently. "Melinda?" She does not respond, and her skin is cold. I withdraw in horror, but not before I see her breasts, how big the nipples are when I know they weren't before.

It's because they're gone.

In their place, ragged wounds. Dark, bloody holes.

Bile floods my mouth.

"You uncorked her like a fucking bottle of Chardonnay," the sponsor says, chuckling.

I fall to the floor in a quivering heap and the vomit rushes out of me in a torrent. Even in the poor light, I can see how dark it is, how thick. I can taste the copper. I can taste the blood.

"Her blood was the only place left to get alcohol at this late hour," the sponsor says, and I jerk away from him. He is standing beside me now, looming over me. I can't run. The strength has left me. I am overcome with horror, with shame. He pats my head like a master will a loyal hound. "You drank it all, drained the bottle. Just like always."

I start to shake my head, the tears rushing in to blind me against what I have done, what he, what *we* have done, and he grabs my hair.

"Closing time," says the sponsor, and rams my face into the locker beside the bed hard enough to shatter the door.

* * *

"Hey, buddy, I said we're closing. Time to get gone."

I raise my head from the bar and open my eyes. Only one of them obeys. The other is swollen shut. A fight, probably. My face is all cuts and bruises. My face is a rubber mask that has tightened in the heat. My skull feels as if someone has filled it with broken glass.

"Hey," I say to the bartender, waving a hand to get his attention. He's at the far end of the bar, sweeping up, a big man, all hair and gut and attitude. "What happened to me?" I indicate my face and the bloodstains on my shirt.

"Fucked if I know," he says gruffly. "You came in here like that. Now, I'd appreciate it if you'd make your exit."

"Bottle for the road?"

He sighs. "You got no money, remember? Spotted you your last round because you looked like you had a bad night, but I'm all out of charity and I'd like to get home sometime tonight, so, if you please, *vaminos*."

I push away from the bar and all the sites of pain register in my brain at once, as if I'm a human Christmas tree. I've gotta stop. I don't know where I am. I barely know who I am, and this has happened once too often. Tomorrow. A familiar chorus, comforting it its bold insincerity. Tomorrow I'll make the change.

"What time is it?" I ask the barkeep.

"Almost three."

"Okay." I slide off the stool and almost collapse in a heap. "Sorry, sorry."

My path to the door is uneven, as if the tavern is aboard a listing ship. Outside, the air is cold, and I shiver, squint against the emptiness of the night. The stars look like glints in the eyes of predators. My chest aches. My stomach is full of acid. My mouth tastes as if I have been sucking on pennies. I look at my watch and find only a pale band of skin where it used to be. Must have lost it, or, more likely, sold it. Doesn't matter because time doesn't matter.

On an otherwise deserted street, a cab cruises by, and I raise an arm and give it a limp wave. I'm surprised when he stops, and hurry into the car, glad to be in out of the cold, which has sobered me, but not nearly enough, and not for long. The leather seat is cold on the backs of my legs. My head throbs.

"Where you going?" asks the driver. He's of ethnic descent and seems tired of me already. That's okay. He can join the fucking club.

"Nearest open bar."

The driver gives me a sigh and a shrug. "Sunday morning. No place open now."

I sit back and appraise him. I can smell his aftershave. It is not unpleasant. He turns around to look at me, thick eyebrows raised questioningly.

"Liquor store then."

"Buddy, no liquor store open now."

I glance longingly back at the bar. The outside lights go off, plunging us into darkness, but not before I catch sight of the figuring standing there on the sidewalk. He doesn't want me to get out of the cab. Doesn't want me to leave. For him, for us, the night has just begun. I feel a flutter of panic in my stomach. Or is it excitement?

"Do you have anything to drink?" I ask the cab driver and he looks at me as if I'm mad.

Of course he won't have anything, but it never hurts to check.

"Sir, I must ask you to leave now. I have to make money, ok?"

The driver is growing restless, cautious.

I don't move.

Can't.

The cab driver has no drink, but he has money. And that will do for now, because I need to find somewhere to be, need to find a part of the city that lives after dark, just like I do. And that kind of living comes with a price. Sometimes it's cash, sometimes a watch, sometimes it's blood. Whatever it takes to satisfy the need.

"Mister, please? I need to go now, you understand?"

I am hit with the sudden urge to ask the driver to bring me home, but I don't know where that is. I know where it should be, where I belong and with whom, but that life seems so very far away, so unattainable. For now, at least. The sponsor promises it is something we can work up to.

Outside the car, the sponsor lights a cigarette, and rotates his free hand, indicating his impatience. *Get on with it.*

"I understand."

There is plenty of darkness still left and we are still alive.

And so

goddamn

thirsty.

THE NO ONE: A RHYME

Somewhere there's a dripping
Somewhere there's a sigh
Someone told me come here
No one told me why

Upstairs there's a scratching
Of nails against the floor
Upstairs there's a weeping
The trying of a door

Downstairs there's a cellar
Downstairs there's a voice
Muttering of sins and deeds
And how it had no choice

Outside there is nothing
Outside's already gone
Inside I am waiting
Inside I am wrong

In here there is darkness
In which I know I'll die
In here I'm the no one
Who wouldn't tell me why

WE LIVE INSIDE YOUR EYES

YOU HAVE NOTHING TO FEAR FROM ME

IN THE END, DESPITE THE PERPETUAL ADMONISHMENTS of her dead mother, Amantha, as she had innumerable times before, made her decision based not on logic but aesthetic appeal. This time, however, it was not just the guy's good looks, but his name which prompted her to quit chewing her lower lip in indecision and finally hit the reply button after an hour of scrolling through his pictures and analyzing his profile. His name was August Windham.

August, she marveled. She had never encountered anyone with that name before. There was Augustus McCrae, the ill-fated hero of *Lonesome Dove*, her favorite novel, but that was a fictional character. *August Windham.* It sounded almost regal, and though wild dogs would never have dragged such an admission out of her, she couldn't help imagining how both names would look on wedding invites: *August and Amantha.* Thus, despite her dear departed, if still overbearing mother's chastisement that she was being typically foolish and impulsive, she wrote the mysterious Mr. August an email expressing interest, and once it was sent, spent the better part of the next two hours cleaning her apartment and feigning calm. Six times she reordered the throw pillows on her couch. She ran the dishwasher twice even though it had only been a quarter full to begin with. She made her bed and then wrecked it just to make it again. Her extensive library of books got a dusting.

Finally, she closed her eyes and took a breath and told herself she was being childish (her mother's disembodied voice concurred) as if the promise of a date had somehow forced her to regress to the cute idiocy of her teens.

To ground herself, she went to the mirror over the bathroom sink.

Her reflection showed bright blue eyes sparkling with hope and excitement, cheeks flushed, her not-quite-full lips spreading into a pleased smile that showed white and almost even teeth. A hand flew to her mouth to conceal the pleasure. She was embarrassing herself, but really, what was so wrong about having a little fun? Her fifty-third birthday was just around the corner—December 18th, to be precise—and if she wanted to send a harmless little "I like you" message off into the ether, perhaps in the fragile hope that the very handsome Mr. August might see it and decide she was worth chasing, then why the hell not? She was a grown woman, and yes, she could admit that there was some validity to her mother's claims that she was given to folly when it came to matters of the heart, but wasn't everyone? Dating was a lottery, nowadays more than ever before, but at least it came with a chance to win, whereas being alone was a loser's game. Of course, there was a problem with that analogy too, for hadn't both of her marriages taught her that being alone can sometimes be the better and happier option? Or, in the case of her first marriage, the *safer* option?

She rolled her eyes at her reflection. "I'm human," she said, indignantly. "And humans make mistakes. It's part of what we are, and I have more than earned the right to make mine, when and however I wish."

She ran a hand through her wavy auburn hair, turned her head this way and that, admiring. Though some had claimed that her angular face and high cheekbones gave her a severe look, she knew she looked good for her age and, if her mother had been any indication, would continue to look good well into her dotage.

"Yes, dear, but I used my years much more wisely than you have."

Amantha straightened her back, pushed her breasts forward, and raised her chin. "That," she told her mother indignantly, "is a matter of opinion."

All composure fled when her computer chimed to indicate a message received.

One last look at herself in the silvered glass, as if the sender of that email might somehow be able to see, and worse, judge her through the screen, and she hurried back into the living room, all nerves.

It's probably just an email from the book club, she told herself, heart pounding in her chest. *Or Judith from the library letting me know they have the new Caroline Kepnes book in.*

But it was none of these things.

As she sat down at the computer, she saw against the background of an Italian villa in summer (her dream escape), the little blue envelope flashing in the bottom right hand corner of the screen. It was from PerfectMatch.com. The subject line read: "Re: Hello, Mr. August."

Breath held, the cold winter light through the tall window behind her creating a dark likeness of herself on the computer screen, she opened the email.

His response read:

Hi Amantha (what a great name!):

Thank you for your message. I must admit it was much more eloquent than I have come to expect on this site. And thanks too for the kind words about my pictures. I'm the worst person to judge what I look like and, combined with my lack of talent with a camera, I worried that they come across as forced or just foolish. On the subject, I am quite taken with your pictures, the quality of which put mine to shame. Clearly you know what you're doing, and you look terrific in them. I particularly liked the one of you on the park bench in the fall. Is that Highbanks? Something about autumn colors makes me warm inside.

Anyway, rather than prattle on, let me say that yes, I am very interested in chatting with you and maybe getting to know each other better. I know too that sites such as these present very real dangers and risks for people, so I'm all for doing whatever I can to assure you of my legitimacy and sincerity. While it's easy to say so, you have nothing to fear from me. Ultimately, I think it would be great to meet you in person, but for now, I am quite happy to know more about you.

I'm glad you got in touch. I noticed your picture before but was a little too shy to pull the trigger. I'm happy you had no such qualms ☺.

Hope to talk soon.

Yours,

August

Amantha read the letter at least two dozen times and studied the half dozen or so pictures of her new flame before she clapped her hands together, rose from her seat and danced her way through the apartment. Always, when she felt most alone, she wished she had a cat or a dog, or even a bird with whom to share such joyous occasions, but now that hardly seemed to matter. The girls in the book club would be thrilled for her, even if they forever operated at a remove from her notion of friendship. Their elation would be tempered by the same distance Amantha had felt from women her whole life without ever knowing its genesis.

"It's because you're odd," her dead mother chimed in. "And they have never once thought you weren't making it up." As usual, she sounded bored, pious, possessed as she had been in life of an unwavering certainty that the nature of all things was no more and no less than she said they were. "I'm sorry, but it's true. You dress strange, you act strange, you *are* strange, and normal people don't know what to do with that. They will be happy for you, sure, because they are nice people. They will also wait for the inevitable heartbreak when it all falls to pieces as it always does and brace themselves for your unique way of dealing with sorrow, which is of course, oddly. I often blamed myself for that, wondered what I could have done differently, but in the end, I cleansed myself of blame once I came to believe that you are the way you are because you simply decided you wanted to be."

Mid-pirouette, Amantha shook her head and closed her eyes. "Say whatever you want, Mother. You can't take away from how I'm feeling. Not today. Maybe not ever again."

"That's fine, dear. Mind me when I say this new euphoria will hardly last very long."

"Says you."

"More than me have said it. You're strange. Compulsively drawn to impossibilities."

"Shut up, Mother. For once just shut up."

Amantha blew air through her lips and headed for the computer desk, a cheap if elegant pine affair with a duo of drawers and sturdy, curved legs. Gingerly, so as not to disturb the contents, she slid open the left-side drawer. Inside, arranged end to end so they made a perfect triangle, were three cigarettes. Pall Malls. All that remained of a habit that had ended up escalating a hereditary blood pressure problem resulting in a week in hospital for what she had suspected was a heart attack. It wasn't. The doctor, in his infuriatingly condescending tone, had told her it was a panic attack, but that quitting was always a good idea if she wanted to live longer. She had held onto these last three cigarettes strictly for celebrations that required more than her customary dancing and defiance of her mother. In the center of the triangle was a red Bic lighter. She freed it and then removed one of the cigarettes. Breaking the triangle pained her on a deeper level than she'd expected, even though she felt it justified. It was not guilt at indulging in something that was bad for her health (and had killed her father) or undoing over a year of abstinence. No, it was simply the act of changing the shape that had sat there in darkness, untouched and unviolated for so long. It felt like wanton destruction of a carefully organized construct. It felt like she should have left it alone, because the triangle, even though she had created it, wanted to be the shape it was.

She screwed the cigarette between her lips and lit up. "Sorry," she said, but reminded herself that all it would take to make the shape whole again would be to replace the missing cigarette, something she resolved to do on her next trip to the store. But this presented another problem. The store didn't sell single cigarettes. She would have to buy a pack, and if she bought a pack then she would have to figure out something to do with all those *other* cigarettes. She wouldn't smoke them. Throwing them away would feel like a waste. Give them away? Wouldn't that be assisting someone else in harmful behavior?

She was getting annoyed, and that wasn't good. Plus, it was hardly the time. Cigarette clamped between her teeth, the smoke curdling in her throat, she waggled her mouse to wake up her computer screen, and, smiling, began to type a response to Mr. August Windham.

* * *

"You know nothing about this man," her mother said.

"Neither do you," Amantha snapped, irritated that the dress she had bought seemed snugger now than it had in the changing room back at the store. Her breasts were hardly big enough to cause obstruction, and yet she found the material hung oddly from them, as if she had purchased the dress solely because it created an overhang from her chest to hide her stomach. And while her stomach was hardly supermodel flat, nor was she ashamed of it. Certainly, it wasn't something she felt warranted concealment and she didn't care to give that impression. Flushed, she shimmied out of the dress and, hands on hips, red dress lying on the floor like a felled and bloody ghost, she inspected herself in the bedroom mirror.

"You're getting pudgy, just like all the women on your father's side of the family," said her mother.

"Oh, shut up. Even death hasn't cured you of your jealousy and bitterness. Doesn't it ever get old?"

But she knew her mother was right, knew that the voice was simply her own impression of her mother's disapproval, which meant that she was admitting her own flaws and insecurities to herself. Projecting such thoughts onto the face of another made them easier to bear, easier to deny, and over time it made the voice real. Sometimes, she thought it might be more real than her own.

"You're going to spend all this time fretting about getting those small tits and big hips into a dress you knew back at the store wouldn't work, all so you can impress some stranger who'll probably turn out at worst to be a rapist, and at best, another in a long line of your failures."

Angrily, Amantha bent down and yanked her dress up off the floor. Like blood through a vein, she worried herself through the outfit and emerged out the other side surer than ever that it would not only fit, but look devastatingly good on her. Briefly, she closed her eyes and smoothed her hands over the bigger wrinkles in the material, focusing on the areas around her breasts, belly and hips, as if she could, simply by wishing it so, mold them into the shape dictated by the label on the dress, the same shape the mirror in the store had claimed she already was.

"You're fooling yourself," her mother said.

Amantha opened her eyes.

"Shut up, Mother."

The woman in the mirror smiled at her, and she looked *good*.

* * *

She was late to the restaurant, a development caused in part by her war with the dress and in another by her inability to locate the place. Her car's GPS had twice led her around in circles, forcing her to park off the street and navigate in treacherous high heels a series of labyrinthine alleys until she saw the warm wedge of light cast upon the cobblestones from an unseen window. Closer and the mullioned window came into view and with it, the subdued murmur of a pleasantly full room. The frontage of the place suggested history, class, and secrecy. It was to her wonder that she had never even heard of the place before, but then, she didn't consider herself much of a foodie and was just as content (if not more) with a greasy pizza or a gyro from one of the neighborhood joints as she was with a high-priced steak at an upscale eatery. Still, as she made her awkward way over the cobblestones toward the restaurant, she felt a flutter of excitement in her chest. The place suggested intimacy, warmth, and pleasure. And, bonus, if it all went to hell, nobody would know her here.

Inside she found herself further seduced by the décor and ambience. Like most high-class places, the class itself was evident even while the menu remained a mystery. No plastic crabs on the walls or fishing nets suspended from the ceiling here. No large chalkboard menus or advertisements for happy hour touting the city's best margaritas or offering cheap shots till 8. No multitude of television screens designed to hypnotize the patrons into watching them. No cheap sticky carpet. No harried looking wait staff dropping their plastic smiles once they'd turned their backs on their tables. Rather, it was, as she'd suspected, small, quiet, warmly lit, and cozy. She estimated there were perhaps a dozen tables, no more, unless there was another section of the place she couldn't see from the door, but somehow, she doubted that. The sole concession to the season was a small and radiantly lit Christmas tree by the bar. The well-dressed staff seemed confident and efficient without need to hurry. The hostess seemed genuinely pleased to see her.

"How are you this evening, Ma'am?"

"Great," Amantha replied, and meant it. Already this felt like something from a dream, or one of the romantic fantasies she often read and intended someday to write.

"Are you meeting someone?"

"Yes, a Mr. August Windham." As suspected, she liked how the name sounded when spoken aloud.

The hostess moved behind her pulpit and consulted a list. For a moment, watching the girl's brow furrow in concentration, she felt a twinge of unease and uncertainty. What if he wasn't here? What if he had stood her up, deciding at the last moment that maybe the woman in those pictures wasn't really that attractive after all? What if some other woman had stolen his attention from her in the two weeks since they'd first made contact, perhaps someone better looking, someone more confident, with more money, someone who didn't need to fool herself into pretending her expensive dress fit the way it was supposed to? The unease started to drift toward panic, fumbling up inside her from belly to chest to throat. It started to get harder to breathe, as if the air had abruptly filled with smoke. She coughed into her fist, felt a single bead of sweat trickle coldly out from beneath her armpit and trickle its way down her side, leaving gooseflesh in its wake.

"Didn't I tell you your silly girlish fantasies would make a fool of you again?" her mother muttered coldly in her ear.

But then the hostess looked up and beamed at her, and that smile was like a blast of heat, killing the chill in one wave. "Right this way, Ma'am." She turned and led the way, pausing to guide Amantha down a small series of steps into the dining room. And as the hostess moved ahead, Amantha scanned the dimly lit room for the man she had come here to see.

She felt a surge of excitement at the sight of him rising from the table to meet her. He was not, as her mother had whispered from the moment she had agreed to meet him, a fraud, an imposter, someone pretending to be someone else. Even in the limited view afforded him by the mood lighting, he was, as his pictures had shown, handsome. "Debonair" was the word she had conjured up when she saw the one of him in the tux at some function or another. His hair was dark and slicked back, his teeth an orthodontist's dream. He was anachronistically handsome, like an old movie star. His eyes glimmered with delight as the hostess deposited her at the table.

"Your server will be with you in a moment," the hostess said, and was gone.

"You made it," August said, and the look of genuine pleasure at the sight of her threatened to melt her on the spot. She felt as if her whole body was full of butterflies.

"Just about," she said, feeling suddenly self-conscious standing there before him. She was not quite sure what to do with herself, her limbs apparently receiving instructions from a quartet of masters.

"Please, sit," he said, and she did.

And from that moment on, with the piped in piano music playing at a low volume from speakers nestled unobtrusively in the shadows, it was as if they had known each other all their lives. The unease fled as quickly as it had come. She relaxed into the evening as if the air itself had become wine. Even her mother had little to say throughout the course of their meal of goat cheese ravioli, King Crab-stuffed sea bass, and afterward, a dual course of crème brûlée, all washed down with a fine Merlot.

Later, over coffee, with the hour growing late and the restaurant all but empty, but with neither one of them inclined to make a move, Amantha knew two things at once. First, she did not believe in love at first sight, and second, she was somehow, inexplicably and wonderfully *in* love at first sight. And while her mother might have always felt like she had raised a fool for a daughter, Amantha did not believe that the man across the table from her was putting her on or engaging in a charade for the sole objective of taking her home. He was too present in the moment, too engaged for it to be anything but real, and that only inflamed her burgeoning passions further. She did not believe she had anything to fear from him, an increasingly rare quality in men these days.

"I just realized I never asked what you do for a living," he said, stirring cream and sugar into his coffee.

"I work from home as a medical transcriptionist," she told him, though it was not quite the truth. She had worked in that field when she needed the money, but with alimony and her inheritance, she hadn't needed to work for a long time. It would not, however, do to admit such a thing upfront.

He took a sip of his coffee and appraised her anew. "Really?"

"Yes, why?" Had the lie been so apparent?

He shrugged. "I would have thought curator at a museum or gallery owner, or something along those lines. You look like you work in the arts."

She leaned forward, eagerly. "Oh, I've always wanted to. I love the arts, in all its forms. Books and painting especially. It just never really panned out for me. I never had the discipline, or the concentration needed for it."

"I would think the best kind of art comes from chaos."

"I suppose it does." It was impossible to keep the smile from her face. The fondness she felt for this man, his voice, his words, his looks, even the scent of him, was unlike anything she had ever felt before and she couldn't keep from broadcasting it across the table to him with every look and gesture. Her mother was in her skull somewhere, pacing, chiding her to abide by the rules of etiquette, meant, not just for respectable women, but for those who wished not to be murdered by charming psychopaths. But though she confessed to a certain degree of naivete over the years—the same which had led to two disastrous marriages and equally as many bad dates—she knew in the core of her being that this man was not going to hurt her. She could sense it. *You have nothing to fear from me*, he had said, and she believed him.

"Honey," her mother said, for once, not unkindly, "I love you, but sense has never been your strong suit. In fact, the absence of that very thing has led to some of your greatest miseries. Please, just be careful."

Amantha shut her eyes and cut off her mother's voice as easily as if it had been carried to her via an old radio.

"Are you all right?" August asked.

August and Amantha. "Oh yes. Just enjoying the atmosphere, although I think the wine has me a little buzzed."

"Should I take you home?"

She opened her eyes and looked at his face for intent. Had he meant he would see her home in the most gentlemanly sense, or go home with her to extend the evening? The longer she looked at him and bathed in their combined aura and all it promised, she realized it didn't matter one way or another. Sooner or later, they would become one.

Thus, when the night ended with their candle the sole light in a sea of growing dark as the restaurant began to close, she let him take her by the arm. On the way out, she exchanged a glance with the pretty hostess who had been so sweet to her before, and fancied she saw some envy there. Perhaps a soupçon of curiosity too. No bitterness, just a wistful longing to share in the same kind of magic that Amantha had found. Amantha was no stranger to that longing.

"Good night," she said to the girl, with a wink and a smile. The hostess was young and beautiful. She had her whole life ahead of her, and though she might have to navigate a minefield to get there, and her dreams would lose some of their color, one day she would find good love too. Amantha was sure of it.

"Good night," said the hostess.

Amantha let August lead her from that place and out into the night. She could feel the warmth of him, could smell the scent of him. It was as intoxicating as the wine. He could take her wherever he wished. She had decided this for him. Tonight, and forever. And when she looked into his handsome, smiling face to convey this to him, she could see he already knew. But he walked her to her car and bid her farewell anyway, because as promised, he was a gentleman and unlike all the others, she had nothing to fear from him. When he made to turn away, she put a hand on his wrist to halt him. He looked back and she closed the distance between them.

The kiss was Heaven and a promise of all the good things to come.

* * *

"Christ, I thought she was never going to leave." Barry slid home the bolts on the big main door of the restaurant.

"I think it's kinda sweet," the hostess said.

"Sweet? She's fucking nuts."

"You have no heart, Bryan."

"I have eyes, Holly. Sometimes that's enough. And I know a fruit bat when I see one."

"Well, I thought it was adorable."

"Why?"

She shrugged. "I just do." She knew better than to try to make him understand. And maybe she wasn't even sure herself why she found the woman so inspiring. Yes, she was odd, acting as though she hadn't been seated at a table she herself had booked while ordering and eating dinner for two. But still, the look of serenity on her face had brought a smile to Holly's. The woman had seemed so comfortable, so secure and so happy dining alone. And then later, as she'd walked out, arm crooked as if linked through that of a phantom lover, the look she had given Holly was one she figured it was going to take a long time to forget.

I am safe, it said. *I hope someday you will be too.*

THE MONSTER UNDER THE BED

"DAAAAAAD!"
"Fuck sake."
"DAAAAAAAAAD!"
"Jesus *Christ*, Billy, *what*?"
"You said a bad w—"
"What do you want now?"
"There's something under the bed."
"Go to sleep."
"There's a monster."
"No, there isn't."
"There is. I heard it."
"It's your imagination, now for the last goddamn time, go to sleep."
"Check."
"What?"
"Check under there, please."
"No. I already told you there's nothing under there. I thought we were through with all this bullshit? You're almost ten years old. Time to stop being such a scaredy-cat. I swear, between you and your mother, it's a wonder I haven't lost my mind already."
"I'm not a scaredy-cat."
"Yes, you are. Only scaredy-cats think there are monsters under their beds."

"I'm not scared."

"Then why don't you look and see for yourself?"

"I want you to do it. Please, just look under there."

"There's no need. I can see from here that there's nothing there but some toys and your dirty laundry. Which, by the way, you were supposed to clean up over the weekend. Now, I'm going to bed and you're going to sleep. It's been a shit day, and I have to be up for work in a few hours."

"Okay, fine."

"Really? You're gonna sulk now? Jesus."

"I'll go to sleep and promise not to bother you again if you just make sure there's nothing there."

"Fine. Christ. Fine. But if you call me again, you'll be sorry."

"Okay."

"Now, see? There's nothing under your goddamn bed. See? Look.

"Oh, but there is, you fucking ogre."

"The *fuck* did you just s—what the? Billy, woah...woah...hey...what are you doing with that? Put that down right this goddamn m—JESUS CHRIST! No, no, NOOOOO. Please, I n—"

"*Now* the monster's under my bed."

"P...please...Bil....Billy....please...call....call an....am....."

"Right back where it belongs."

THE HOUSE ON ABIGAIL LANE

THE EARLIEST KNOWN DISAPPEARANCE IS THAT of fifty-eight-year-old Elmore Washington during the construction of the house in June of 1956. Then, as now, there was little to distinguish Number 56 from the twenty-two identical houses that comprised the newly built neighborhood of Abigail Lane. And on that fine summer day sixty years ago, it was starting to come together nicely. The air was punctuated by the bark of hammers and the growl of saws, of machinery grumbling, of trucks grinding their way over the as-yet unpaved streets and driveways. A haze of dust hung over everything. The rough framing had been completed, the plywood sheathing applied to the skeletons of the houses, and the doors and windows had been installed.

According to his coworkers, Elmore, who'd been working primarily on the roof that day, hadn't exhibited any noticeable sign of preoccupation. He was known as a jovial, quick-witted sort, slow to anger unless raging drunk, in which case, Jeb Foreman said later, "He'd pick a fight with a chair and probably lose." He was not given to moods or depression. If there were demons nestled in the folds of his life, he kept them to himself. All of which made it even more of a mystery that he, in the middle of an ordinary work day, vanished, and was never seen again. His co-worker Jeb Foreman (who was *not* the foreman, because that would have been a little too perfect) says the last time he saw Elmore, he was entering the house to retrieve his lunch pail, which he'd left somewhere on the second floor. Jeb claimed he saw Elmore mount the stairs ("saw those big size elevens of his clomping up the steps") and didn't give it a second thought until close to quitting time when Ronald Mayhew (who *was* the foreman) asked if Elmore had left early.

Figuring maybe he'd snuck away for a quick nap, they looked for him. On the stairs in Number 56, they found his lunch pail, the bologna sandwich and apple rotted as if it had been sitting in the sun for two weeks, and another item everyone was pretty sure Washington wouldn't have left behind on purpose, which was when it was decided that the police should be called.

All anyone knew was that wherever Washington had gone, he'd traveled there without his car, a 1953 Packard Clipper, parked at the construction site, and eighty dollars' worth of savings he'd kept in a Mason jar beneath his bed. He had never married, wasn't known as "a ladies' man" on account of badly pockmarked skin and a glass eye, so he left no broken hearts behind, only a mother who suffered from dementia and likely died never knowing he'd disappeared.

What he *did* leave behind, was the eye, which Jeb and Ronald discovered sitting on the second to last step of the stairs. "That thing put the fear of God into me," Ronald said. "Like that Poe story about the fella with the big eye, looking at that man like it knew all he'd done." Jeb said he felt sick after emerging from the house. "For some reason I can't figure, I couldn't stop clenching my teeth. The air was all wrong in there. I smelled fresh cut grass, and there ain't a thing wrong with a smell like that, but it made me sick to my stomach." Before he lost his lunch on the bare earth of the soon-to-be lawn, Jeb told his wife he could have sworn he saw sunflowers there, just for a moment, right where someone in the future would undoubtedly put them. He made her promise she'd never share what he said. "The men will think I've gone soft in the head." And she didn't, until the documentarian Mike Howard came calling some six years after lung cancer made her a widow.

Of all the theories put forth at the time to explain what had become of Washington, which ranged from the possible (he'd been suffering from depression and, to spare his mother, had committed suicide somewhere the body was not likely to be discovered), to the highly improbable (he was a Communist sympathizer who'd been called back to Mother Russia for an important assignment)—nobody blamed the house.

II

Despite the dilapidation, Number 56 does not appear sinister at all, at least, no more than any house that has fallen into ruin. Of course, for those who want to characterize the building as a Seething House of Evil, the missing shingles, boarded up windows, and the sagging roof is ample fodder. Similarly, the smoke stains on the façade and the smudges of soot around the windows—testament to an attempt to burn the place to the ground back in 1988—make it look sad, tortured, cursed, to those who wish to regard it that way.

I imagine it looked anything but sad back in the winter of 1957 when the Wilson Family took up residence.

Harold Wilson was an insurance salesman from Skokie, Illinois. Due to a shift within his company (he would have died before he'd admit it had anything to do with his own poor performance), he was relocated to Columbus, Ohio. To ease the sting of what was essentially a banishment, Sun Life & Liberty Provincial provided him with the house on Abigail Lane. Had they foreseen the consequences of this action, or had Wilson been aware of the disappearance of poor Mr. Washington eight months earlier, an alternate residence might have been arranged. But without knowing what had become of the construction worker, and with nobody left behind to ask questions, Washington's vanishing was relegated to *one of those things.*

Thus, unburdened by disappearances past, Harold moved into Number 56 on January 1st of that year with his wife Alison and their children, May, who was eight years old, and Bud, who was twelve.

Despite the circumstances that forced Harold to uproot his beloved family and haul whatever belongings they could fit into his father's old Dodge pickup truck three hours south to a city he didn't know, Harold quickly warmed to Columbus. He bonded with the neighbors over football, and Alison, never the social butterfly, suddenly had more friends than she knew what to do with. Visitors to the house were common, and their calendar quickly filled with events to keep them occupied and ingratiate them further into their new surroundings. Even more surprising, Harold thrived at the new office, a development he put down to the clean slate in a place in which he felt less jaded. Customers seemed more responsive to him and his sales improved.

The kids too seemed happy, though Bud had some trouble at school, whereas May, ever the precocious one, slotted right in as her parents knew she would. Shy and reserved, "a thinker rather than a talker" as his father was fond of telling the neighbors, Bud continued to keep to himself, except when challenged. After the resident bully made fun of Bud's prominent front teeth and shock of ginger hair on the second day, Bud gave him a black eye and a split lip and was henceforth left alone. Bud weathered the inevitable lecture the same way he always did in the wake of these curious outbursts of violence: he stared down at his lap and rubbed his hands together as if washing them. Alison found Bud impenetrable and worrisome, but Harold was secretly proud. He himself had never been a fighter, only a victim (the relocation being just the latest in a long line of humiliations at the hands of others), and it buoyed him to know that in that regard at least, his son was not going to follow in his footsteps. As it turned out, the only footsteps in which Bud was destined to follow were those of Elmore Washington, because on the night of February 10th, 1957, a little over six weeks after they moved into their new house, young Bud clomped upstairs to bed and was never seen again.

Nobody would have sold the house to the Wilsons if they'd known that something was wrong with it. Or perhaps they would. Greed is a great motivator, and the real estate market is loaded with houses of ill repute and unscrupulous realtors, because at the end of the day, to anyone who doesn't believe in the supernatural, a house is just a house, and people will always need someplace to live. Besides, Number 56 had not yet earned its dark reputation. It will come as no great surprise given certain realities at the time that the disappearance of Elmore Washington, a black man, never made the news. To the few people who knew him, he was just a lonely unremarkable man bound for a lonely, unremarkable end, and that's exactly what he got, however he came upon it.

However, because he was white, and because he was a middle-class child with a bright future ahead of him, the disappearance of Bud Wilson got plenty of attention. Less than a half hour after Harold—never Harry—checked in on the kids and found Bud's room empty, a pair of policemen were at his door. An hour after that, a search was underway, but all they turned up was one of his shoes, which he could have kicked off on the way to bed, though the absence of the second one did raise questions.

Bud would forever be convinced that someone had been waiting in the boy's room and had snatched him, though to do so, the would-be abductor would have had to sneak a struggling kid downstairs and through the living room where Harold and his wife were watching *The Ed Sullivan Show*, which Harold insisted (perhaps because he'd never have been able to live with it if it were true) was not the case. But the single window in the boy's room was still latched, which ruled out egress via that route. The theory favored by police was that there had been no abductor at all, at least not inside the house, and the boy had simply snuck past his parents and out the front door. Where he'd been going or what he might have been up to would remain a mystery, but as time went on, most everyone agreed that whatever the boy's plans had been, they did not lead him to a benevolent end.

At the time, nobody mentioned that the boy was not the first to go missing from the house. Without knowing the fate of Washington, who for all anyone knew had simply quit to go on a bender, raising that connection might be seen, per the notorious statement of Detective Alan Hopper, as "muddying the waters." [Much has been written about the history of Abigail Lane, specifically how racial bias and outright prejudice plagued the investigation from the first, so I won't rehash it here, but if you can find "The One You Didn't See", Margaret Haywood's terrific *NY Times* article on the subject, it makes for a compelling, and depressing, read.]

But now, the young son of a stalwart nuclear family was missing and the police left no stone unturned in their search. So many flyers were tacked to poles, you couldn't travel a hundred miles in any direction without seeing the kid's black and white mug grinning back at you. The media were all over it, and why wouldn't they? The way they saw it, a wholesome freckled-faced young white boy, emblematic of the hope of our great nation, had gone astray, and Lord, oh Lord, must he be found.

Well, he wasn't found. Not only that, but two years to the day Bud vanished, his father did too. By itself, this development might not have been so sensational, except that someone was there to *see* the house take him. Thus, it's here, with Harold Wilson, that the supernatural angle finally comes into play, because people go missing all the time, but rarely do they literally vanish into thin air while you're looking at them. Which is, according to Officer Miles Dietrich, exactly what happened. Dietrich would later use the incident as the basis for his book *Cursed House: My Encounter with Abigail*, which was poorly written and full of inconsistencies and false claims. Not that Dietrich cared. All the negative reviews in the world couldn't dampen the appeal of yet another in a long line of "case studies" about supposedly haunted houses. He made a bundle of money when it was released back in 1987, and it's set to become a limited series this fall on Netflix. According to *Entertainment Weekly*, the eighty-seven-year-old is currently working on the sequel, *Return to Abigail House*. [Somewhere along the line, the house stopped being known by its number—56—and instead became "Abigail House", though that's actually the name of the street, not the house itself.]

But back in 1959, many years before he realized how much he could benefit from embellishing and publicizing his account, here's what he said when interviewed by a reporter from *The Delaware Gazette*:

"I got the call from Mrs. Wilson at about...oh, nine o' clock maybe. She said he'd been drinking. Harold Wilson, that is, and that he was going on and on about the house, saying that it took his boy. Said that the more he thought about it, the more he started to remember. Told her that right before the boy went missing, there'd been a feeling in the air, like someone had opened a big heavy door in the earth beneath the house. He asked her if she remembered that the TV had acted funny right around that time, that there'd been some kind of disruption on the screen that caused Ed Sullivan's face to disappear and made headlights of his eyes. Asked her if she'd smelled the engine oil in the air. She said she thought she might have recalled smelling *something*, but it was more like smoke. When she pleaded with him not to drink any more because the look in *his* eyes was scaring her, he stormed out into the cold without a coat and jumped into his car. He was yelling about the boy, saying he was going to go take him back. That's when she called us. She was afraid he would get himself into an accident. They weren't living but twenty minutes from the house on Abigail. I guess they couldn't bear to live in it any longer but wanted to stay close in case the boy ever found his way back. She figured that's where Harold was going, so that's where I went."

If you've read Dietrich's book, you're about to see just how much that account diverges from the one recorded on the night in question. Here there are no *Poltergeist*-like flashes of light around the house, no seismic tremors or disembodied voices, no feeling of illness once he crosses the threshold. There is nothing but a broken man on the stairs. And that was enough.

"When I got there, the front door was open. Inside, I found Wilson sitting on the stairs with a bottle of bourbon in his hand. He didn't look surprised to see me, but he didn't look pleased either. Just in case, I kept a hand near my gun. He noticed and didn't much like it. He asked if I was going to shoot him. I told him I had no plans to do anything of the kind. His eyes were gone. I don't know how else to say it. They were just empty holes. I've taken fish out of my freezer that had more life in their eyes. 'The house et my boy,' he told me, 'And I want him back.' I said I understood, and to pacify him, proposed we take a good look around the place just to be sure the kid wasn't here. His crooked smile was a terrible thing to witness, like someone had undone a coat hanger and held it up before his face. 'He's not here,' he said. 'He's in the stomach of this place. Being digested so he can come back as something else somewhere else. No, we won't find him here unless we take a walk down its throat.'

"I looked around at the house. Two years without someone living in it had started to take its toll. The windows were busted, the lock on the front door gone, the hallway littered with glass. It was a place of mischief now. [Thus we see the first inklings of Dietrich's penchant for the same purple prose and melodrama which would permeate his first book almost three decades later, though at this point in his *memoir*, he'd already encountered a series of ghostly orbs and heard his dead mother speaking to him from between the cracks in the living room floorboards.] It was sad to see what had become of the place. 'I have to go now,' Wilson said, and when I looked back—and this is the part you're not now or ever going to believe—I saw him rise and turn and put one foot on the step to go upstairs. It creaked, and then...*poof!* He was gone. Just like that, like someone had closed the shades and shadowed him out of being. The bottle he'd been holding in his hand fell from mid-air and smashed against the step. Something else did too. I saw a small flash of light. Heard a faint *ting!* It was his wedding ring. Even though I'd seen a man vanish, disappear like he'd just become fog or something, I told myself I hadn't. Told myself I'd imagined it, or that he was pulling a prank on me. I mean, people don't disappear like that. Not unless they're magicians, right? So I searched for him, and found nothing, just an empty house. Except it didn't *feel* empty. No, the longer I was inside it, the more crowded it started to feel, like there was a whole bunch of people there. So I ran and I'm not proud of it, but I was scared, and anyone who says that makes me a coward didn't see a man blink out of existence right in front of him. And I remember what he said, what he asked his wife. The smell. There was definitely a smell. Jesus, I can still smell it, only it isn't motor oil or smoke. It's roses. I know that smell because my wife grows 'em."

III

The more remarkable claims in Dietrich's statement are, not shockingly, absent from the official police reports. These days you can publish anything and find a receptive audience for it, but in 1959, with neither the Korean War nor the Second Red Scare far enough in the rearview, people were not in the mood for more boogeymen. So the story went that it was not a mysterious unearthly force that had erased Harold Never-Harry Wilson off the face of the earth after all, but grief. The loss of his son had caused the man himself to be lost, and though Alison Wilson refused to believe it, the media, working with information supplied to them by sources within the Columbus Police Department, spun the narrative that Harold had fled his wife in a drunken suicidal rage and Officer Dietrich showed up at the house on Abigail Lane to signs that he'd been there, but little else. The moment Dietrich shared his crazy story with reporters and his superiors, he'd condemned Harold Wilson to death *in absentia*. The investigation was half-hearted at best, and soon the story went away.

Alison grieved and waited for her family to come back to her. When they didn't, she packed up and moved back to Indiana. On a bittersweet note, her losses would make her something of an Internet celebrity in later years as documentarians, parapsychologists, and amateur sleuths sought her out. Despite the painful subject, she seemed to enjoy the attention, and made for a funny and fascinating guest. She was asked to attend innumerable paranormal conventions, but declared that she was too old for such things. Nevertheless, she does appear in *The Haunting of Abigail House*, Mike Howard's sprawling documentary. When she died in her sleep in January of 2017, over 1500 people showed up at her funeral, most of them fans. Howard delivered the eulogy. He lamented that Alison had died not knowing what had become of her family, and vowed not to stop searching until he found out.

It was a promise he did his best to keep.

For almost a decade after Harold Wilson's disappearance, the house on Abigail Lane was quiet. The neighbors did not fear it. Why would they? Bad things happened in every home, and you must remember that they most likely didn't know that Harold Wilson and Elmore Washington had also been vanished by the house. Most of them were only aware of Bud Wilson's disappearance, a tragic event that had left the house an unrentable, unsellable nuisance in an otherwise perfectly put together neighborhood, the one bad tooth in a healthy smile. A few of them even took it upon themselves to keep the yard maintained so it did not become a jungle. Neighborhood kids spun wild stories about the place and broke in after dark. None disappeared, all emerged unscathed, though perhaps not always with their wholesomeness intact.

By 1966 there was a different monster stealing people away: The Vietnam War, and some theorists have speculated that this was the reason the house fell dormant, but I think that's bunk. First, it presupposes that the house has a consciousness and a *conscience*, that it somehow felt bad because chaos was consuming the world elsewhere and so it just decided to quit vanishing people for a while. I don't buy it. Second, we don't actually *know* for sure that it ever stopped. During those insane years when every day must have felt like a giant crater had opened up in the world and they were all slowly sliding down into hell, people would have been much less inclined than usual to notice what was happening on their own doorsteps.

Consider the case of twenty-year-old Sharon Grey.

Sharon stole her father's Studebaker and left her home in Flint, Michigan in the dark of night on September 18th, 1965. She was running away, fed up of her controlling parents. She wanted to be an artist and move to New York. They wanted her to be a nurse. She yearned for hedonism, activism, and the bohemian life she saw nightly on the news. Greenwich village beckoned. So, she took matters into her own hands and lit out for the territories. Maybe she even made it to New York and realized her dream, but if so, she did it without the car, which the police found parked four blocks from Abigail House. But of Sharon, there was no trace. None of the boards had been pried loose from the window of the house, and there were no telltale items on the floor of the stairs to suggest her supernatural removal from the world. The police searched the house, found nothing, and moved on. But all these years later, it seems odd that of all the places to stop between Flint and New York, her car should turn up in a suburb northeast of Columbus, instead of downtown, which would have been the more logical place for a traveler to call it a night. But nobody saw it happen and nobody really cared. The world had bigger concerns. Even her parents didn't seem all that eager to learn her fate. It would later emerge that they viewed their daughter as an embarrassment. She was not, they would say, religious. She was headstrong, disrespectful, and unwilling to follow the path they thought best for her, which led to frequent public arguments that reflected badly upon their family as a whole. It mortified them that she had run away. That she had stolen her father's car to do it rendered her no better than a common thief. Thus, they settled for the fantasy that their errant daughter had found her rightful place among the heathens, homosexuals, and hippies in the cesspit of New York, where if they were lucky, she would stay.

    The next notable event occurred on April 30th, 1966, an unfortunate date that would forever after connect it, and the house, to Anton LaVey's opening of The Church of Satan in San Francisco, which happened on the same day. There are enough websites out there dedicated to forging and discussing theories about these two disparate events, all of them ridiculous, so I won't waste time on them here, but for would-be Satan worshippers or those of a Gothic bent, the iconic imagery of dozens of dogs and cats camped out on the lawn of the house on Abigail Lane, all of them unmoving, all facing the house...well, it's easy to see the appeal, if only for recruitment purposes. The animals got a short writeup in the local rags, little more than a sidebar, but in 1982, in one of her nonfiction pieces for *Analog*, science fiction author Patricia Burr [writing under her nom de plume of J.A. Kennedy to circumvent the sexism so prevalent in publishing at the time], speculated that the animals were lured to the site either by high-frequency soundwaves or a peculiarly strong magnetic field unregistered by humans. She bemoaned the missed opportunity for proper scientific study of the phenomenon, the absence of empirical evidence leaving the door open for decades of preposterous theories, the most prominent and outrageous of them being that the house was recruiting animals for an army to overthrow the human race!

These were animals, something worthy of remark and little else. Like a murmuration of starlings, it was an eerie sight but indicative of nothing, and certainly not worth obsessing over. After a period of three hours and twenty-six minutes in which none of the animals so much as blinked, they snapped out of whatever paralysis had held them in thrall and wandered away. In the years since, many people have brought their pets to the scene in the hope that something similar will happen (surely a form of abuse), but it never has. It seems it was a one-time only party trick, at least as far as the animals are concerned, for we can't forget the Fourth of July weekend of the following year in which seventeen people snapped awake to find themselves standing on the lawn outside the house. It was 2 a.m., most of them were in their pajamas or slips, two were stark naked, all of them were horrified. And now, because people were involved, theories moved into the realm, not of the supernatural, but of the sinister. Whispers of Soviet mind-control experiments, of Communist infiltration, of chemical agents being tested on suburban neighborhoods, of hallucinogens in the water. The Thalidomide tragedy had yet to be forgotten. Who was to say what nefarious experiments the pharmaceutical companies might have moved on to? Perhaps something to make people forget? Mass hypnosis? Doctors were brought in, virologists swept the neighborhood, men in radiation suits with Geiger counters clickety clicked their way from Holden Avenue down through Abigail and out the other side and found nothing untoward. If there was a commonality to be found, it was that the afflicted had nothing but good health, both mental and physical, in common. Everything from abrupt changes in temperature to the proximity of that night to the first of the year's two lunar eclipses was floated as a possible explanation for the sleepwalkers.

Cut to May 21st, 1973. The war is over. Nixon is four months into his second and final term and staring right into the maw of the Watergate scandal. Soldiers come home, not to parades, but suspicion and scorn. Monsters roam the country abducting and murdering children. There is a sense of disorder to the country, of pieces no longer fitting. The relief at the war ending quickly turns to economic anxiety and a distillation of old enmities and grievances. That the president of the United States may be an inveterate liar and all-around archvillain is not a reality for which the nation is prepared.

The external war has become internal, found a way to crawl inside.

And the house comes back to life.

IV

Doug Lowell returned from Vietnam, where he had served as an information specialist, in April of 1973. On May 21st of that year, he moved into the house with his wife Katrina and their three-year old daughter, Serena, who had been born eight weeks after he was deployed.

Doug was a good guy, and smart. He'd seen the kind of horrors most people only see in their nightmares and somehow managed to come home intact. Experts (if it's possible to be an expert on the unknown and unknowable) have nevertheless retroactively diagnosed Lowell with PTSD, a postwar psychological affliction that wasn't recognized as legitimate until after the National Vietnam Veterans Readjustment Study in 1980, seven years after Lowell took possession of the house. It's hard to argue with this stance given that much of what Lowell documented fits under the umbrella of PTSD: hallucinations, paranoia, agitation, hypervigilance, emotional detachment, and fear. Viewed outside the lens of the house's reputation, the papers Lowell wrote only bolster this conclusion. He appears manic, unhinged. Inside it, though, it provides remarkable insight into one possible, and relatively recent theory about what might be going on in the house, put forth, if you can believe it, by Arthur A. Windale, noted conspiracy theorist and UFOlogist, whose book *They're Already Here: Aliens Among Us* caused outright panic among devout believers back in the early seventies. Even if it reads at best like science fiction and at worst, like an anti-communist manifesto, I must confess I found it unexpectedly engaging. I bought none of it, of course, but Windale certainly had an authoritative, declarative style that made it easier to see how those who might want to believe, would. And though we can't pretend his interest in the Abigail case wasn't motivated by money and a need to revitalize his flagging career, Windale's contribution to the fray nevertheless proved intriguing. While his contemporaries were on cable news blathering on about long debunked mysteries like The Bermuda Triangle and the *Marie Celeste*, Windale took the time to research the house.

"When reading back over the history of this place," he wrote in his blog, "certain things stand out in my mind. The smells, for one, a detail that has gone bafflingly unstudied. It sounds like phantosmia, which suggests some manner of magnetic anomaly in the house that induces symptoms more commonly associated with a stroke, or schizophrenia, but my compass remained unmoved, and none of the afflicted subjects developed complications typical of these conditions once they left the house. Jeb Foreman died of cancer, yes, but he was in his nineties and a heavy smoker for two-thirds of those years. Harold Wilson went mad with grief typical of anyone who's lost a son. And while magnetic interference (as suggested by my dear friend Trish [Patricia Burr] scrambling the brain could result in the kind of hallucination necessary to make a man appear to vanish, where then, did Wilson go? Something you *think* you see should not be so easily written off as a trick of the mind. A man did vanish, did he not? When you open and shut a door in the summer, do you not smell the fresh cut grass, or the heat of the asphalt? That's the conclusion I keep coming back to, as impossible as it sounds. A door opened and closed behind these people and we smelled what was on the other side. They are over there, those poor souls, wherever *there* is. Now all we need divine is how to find them."

Like so much of the speculation surrounding the house, and taking into account his record of outlandish claims (such as his theory that the colonists at Roanoke were spirited into a wormhole engineered by aliens and likely deposited on some distant planet), Windale's should have been just as easy to dismiss. And it might have been, if not for Doug Lowell's account of something that happened to him on the night of May 1st, 1983, not even four months after he moved into the house. The following is an excerpt from one of the four essays he wrote for Marita Hopkins & Karun Venkatesh's nonfiction study of combat shock:

I thought I must be dreaming. I remember waking up, bladder full and aching. Katrina was asleep next to me. I could smell the conditioner she uses in her hair. I love that smell and that night, as it so often does, it grounded me in the safe here and the real now. I left her and quietly made my way to the door to Serena's room. So often I've dreamed I would wake up one night and she'd be gone, stolen from us to settle whatever debt I accrued in the jungle. But she was there, safe too, breathing soft and slow. Goaded by my bladder, I moved on, thankful despite the hummingbird hammering of my heart that told me something was awry. Was there someone in the house? The hair prickling all over my body suggested so, but I couldn't trust that alone. My instinct tells me there's always someone there who shouldn't be and there never is. It will pass, I know it will, that certainty, the suspicion that there are people watching me from the walls and that my shadow wishes me harm. I went to look. I did not take my bat. If someone made it past me, I preferred Katrina to have it close by. And I didn't want her waking to see me wielding it. She's already worried enough about me since I got home. I'm worried too. The nightmares. Jesus. It's like someone planted screws inside my head that are slowly worming their way back out. That'll pass too. I have faith, and God owes a debt of his own.

    I reached the top of the stairs and braced myself in the dark for whatever might be waiting down there with a gun, or a knife. I slowed my breathing, demanded my pulse slow too before my heart exploded. I hurried downstairs into the living room...

    ...and the living room was gone.

Immediately I smelled chlorine, that strong summertime pool smell when they put too much of it in the water and it burns the hell out of your eyes. And that pool was in my living room, or rather, where the living room used to be. Now, I found myself outside in a daylit courtyard, the glare of the sun being slapped to pieces by the waves as children laughed and splashed and hollered at their parents, those patiently smiling bronzed-bodied adults lounging in chairs on both sides of the pool. None of them had faces, only thin-lipped mouths, and their hair, all the same light pink color, moved sinuously as if underwater. The dappled light from the pool animated their faces in place of expressions. It felt entirely reasonable to scream when I looked up and away from these impossible monsters and saw misshapen black birds with half a dozen silver dollars for eyes. Their beaks were like bruised human hands snapping from the air insects the size of my fist. I stepped away, my body tensing to run, and collided with a child, who cursed at me in a language I don't know, and then giggled. I did not look at him. Couldn't. Had I seen his face, or the lack of one, I might have lost my mind. I did not look when he called "Olop Ocram!" at me. And I did not linger on the fact that the sinewy faceless man who dove into the pool scattered into a school of pink and silver fish as soon as he went under. No, I kept backing away and whispering the same prayers that went ignored during the war when men caught fire and screamed until their lungs burned and a headless child tumbled from the back of a truck on its way out of a razed village. I backed away now as then and only opened my eyes again when my spine rammed into an obstacle that felt too real to be a dream.

I was home, in the dark, but not alone. The living room was a conspiracy of shadows and among them I could hear a man speaking backwards in a low voice. I did not care to hear him, so I jammed my fists against my ears. I could still smell the chlorine, could only watch as the man rose from behind the armchair where he'd been hiding. Arms outstretched as if for balance, he took one step, then another, and on the third his thick silhouette split in half and then there were two men standing in the room.

A scream barreled up my throat and turned to a mewl in my mouth. My heart pounded against my ribs, a tribal drumbeat demanding an end to this horror before it split in two like the guest who'd followed me home.

I shut my eyes and knew when I looked again, the men would be gone.

But they weren't.

They were right in front of me, standing so close I could smell the sunscreen on their skin. "Ereht rehto eht morf er'uoy," one of them said, his words sluggish bubbles in a clogged sink. "Yats thgim ew." Self-preservation took over and I lashed a clumsy fist in the direction of the nearest one's head. I expected resistance, collision, meat against meat, but realized I should have known better because nothing was normal now. My hand passed through what felt like warm wet jelly that spread across the air in an arc and then stayed there like a swipe of paint on a windshield. "Yllis," said the undamaged one, and then both fell to the floor like dropped coats.

My breathing sounded like the last exhalations of a snared jackrabbit. I did not dare move even when the sun rose and filtered through the blinds, even when Katrina found me, her face pallid with concern, even when I finally looked down and saw the puddle of piss on the floor at my feet. I did not move.

I still don't want to.

* * *

Lowell sought out a therapist after that. She assured him his imagination was to blame for the incident he described above, that he'd experienced a night terror, an expected consequence of his exposure to the horrors of war. As he could hardly argue with the definition of what he'd experienced, he embraced it as the diagnosis. His doctor prescribed diazepam, and when six months passed without incident, he was happy to accept his therapist's version of events. The conjurations of a haunted mind, and nothing more. Nevertheless, on Christmas Eve of the same year, the night he would pack his family into their Country Squire Station Wagon and drive nonstop until they reached his sister's place in Madison, Wisconsin, the house delivered onto him another unpleasant surprise, and this time Doug's wife was there to see it:

That last night, the last good night, Katrina and I were on the sofa, watching a Christmas movie. I can't remember which one, only that it was an oldie. We were happy. I remember that because it was the last time. The fire was blazing and though the weatherman told us not to expect snow, we did anyway. We wanted it to. It was all that was missing. The house was profusely decorated. Tinsel wreathed the tree. The multicolored lights blinked slowly on and off. We were looking forward to the morning and the small selection of gifts we'd wrapped for Serena, and each other.

Then, my ears popped, and Katrina wrinkled her nose. "What is that smell?" she asked. I started to tell her I didn't know what she was talking about, but then my nose filled with the odor of popcorn and sawdust. She sat up and looked around, and I told myself it was nothing to get worked up about. Popcorn, for goodness sake. What kind of a man loses his nerve over that?

The knock on the door made Katrina scream, and my heart became a cold hard rock in my chest. Her smile chased it away. "Carolers," she said. "It must be."

"This late?" I asked, but she was already up and moving toward the door. Dread fell over me like a shroud. That feeling was back, the same one I'd had on that night when The Backward Men followed me home. "Honey, don't—"

Despite the paralysis threatening to turn my limbs to stone, I rose as she opened the door onto an absence of carolers. She turned to look at me, questioning, and then her gaze moved past me to the stairs. I didn't want to look. Seeing the color drain from her face and her eyes bulge in horror was enough. We needed to go, to run, to hide, to be as far away from here as we could get before the gas ran out.

"Oh..." was all she said, and I watched her back into the door, slamming it shut behind her, trapping us with whatever was in the room.

"What is it?" I asked, but didn't want to know, even though the not knowing was even worse. Was something bearing down on me with claws raised to flay me?

Unwillingly, I glanced over my shoulder.

On the stairs was a ten-foot clown. He was dressed in a tattered costume and stooped over to avoid cracking his head on the slanted ceiling. In one hand he held a smoking umbrella, the edges burnt black, as if it had been struck by lightning. In the other hand, he held a dog collar.

"You see it?" I asked my wife, and from the corner of my eye, saw her nod.

"What...is it?"

I had no answer. Nobody would ever know what that thing was. Its hair was electricity, arcing and sparking and dancing around its raw red peeling skull. At first, I thought it had bandages wrapped around its face until it looked toward my wife and I saw the hands and the little fingers moving against its cheek, and realized what I was looking at was a mask made of tiny arms. I needed to look away because I was more frightened than I had ever been before, but I couldn't. Instead I glanced down, looking for a way to rush past it, and saw that beneath the filthy cuffs of its baggy blue polka dot pants, its legs ended in brown serrated spikes, like the leg of an insect.

What should have been comforting, but wasn't, was how it seemed confused by us, confused to find itself here in our house, but ascribing human reactions to such an offensively alien thing would have been a fatal mistake. It looked this way and that, though how it could see anything at all with no apparent eyes was a mystery. Maybe it couldn't.

Then: "Peekabooooooo," it said in a voice like a fistful of pennies being dropped into a glass jar.

"Serena," my wife said, voice strained by tears, and I knew the time for inaction was over. Though petrified, and yes, afraid of dying at the hands of the monstrosity blocking the stairs, I refused to let my own fear keep me from saving my daughter. And if I failed...no, I couldn't fail. I would tear it asunder if it got between me and my little girl. I didn't truly believe this, of course, but the thought was enough to get me moving, even as I registered the chittering sound and the undulating motion beneath the thing's silver and blue jumpsuit. And now there was another sound too: static, repetitive, like a record spinning on an empty groove.

With a hastily whispered prayer, I stepped forward, and an orange light blinked on upstairs, drowning me in the creature's shadow. The clown straightened in surprise and bonked his head against the ceiling. "Oof," he said in that same terrible voice. The electricity bowed and sizzled and sparked. He grunted and looked back over his shoulder at a studio warning sign which had been affixed above the door to our bedroom. In dark red letters it read: CLOWNMANTIS LIVE IN FIVE. He gave a sigh like an autumn wind, looked back at us, those fingers on his face drumming his agitation, and then he turned and lumbered back down the hall. Incredulous, we watched him leave, until the door that only moments before had led to our bedroom, creaked shut behind him and the light went off.

We got our daughter and went to the car, with just the clothes on our backs. I don't care what explanations you might have for what happened to us. Say I imagined it. Say we both did. It doesn't matter. We were never going to set foot in that house again, and I will forever curse the day I bought it.

* * *

For a while, Lowell kept his story to himself. No media, no police reports, no sensationalism. He just upped and left his home, without a word to anyone. But no matter the circumstances for leaving one's abode, mortgage lenders expect to be paid. Lowell would have gone broke paying for the house that had almost driven him insane if not for the kindness of his sister and her husband, who let him stay with them rent-free until his situation improved. He took a part-time job tending bar. Such situations can fracture a marriage, or make chasms of existing ones, and by the fall of 1974, Katrina moved back to Columbus to live with her parents. Doug pleaded with her to stay so he could be with his daughter, but she felt him an unstable influence, and no matter how desperately he wanted to argue, he knew she was right. He let them go, as much as he'd let go of himself.

A few months later, he accepted the offer from a publishing house for a series of essays documenting his experiences with postwar trauma (*An Affliction Without a Name: Combat Shock in the Vietnam Era*, by Marita Hopkins & Karun Venkatesh, Veteran's Day Press, 1976), from which the preceding excerpts were taken. The week after he received his contributor copies in the mail, he left a note tucked inside one of them thanking his sister and her husband for everything, told her to ensure Katrina and Serena knew he loved them and had tried so very hard to be the husband and father they'd needed him to be, and then hanged himself from the limb of the oak tree in his sister's yard.

War, as they say, continues to take its toll long after the last shot has been fired. In Lowell's case, the house on Abigail Lane was instrumental in his undoing.

V

After trying and failing to make Katrina Lowell responsible for the mortgage payments on the abandoned house, the property was foreclosed, then rehabbed (without incident) and prepped for resale in March of 1975.

The realtor charged with reselling it was a forty-three-year-old woman named Sandy Radcliffe from Dayton, Ohio. Sandy worked for Dominion Realty, and was known, not just for her high turnover rate, but for taking a keen interest in the history of the properties she was tasked to sell. She had always thought it prudent to know what she was selling beyond the scant details provided her by the office.

From the beginning, Number 56 gnawed at her. Much of it was Lowell's suicide. Even though it hadn't happened inside the house, he had still been the last to live there, and she wondered what might have driven him to such a tragic end.

Her own younger brother George had died in Vietnam. Her older brother Graham had also served in the marines and had come home changed in ways she struggled to comprehend. Gone was the quick-to-smile gangly kid who'd once pledged to be her "forever protector", who'd given her away at her wedding, and had never failed to call on her birthday and on Christmas. He was so unknown to her now it was as if he'd died over there too. He spent all his time listening to old jazz records and writing lyrics in journals. His room was stacked full of them. He was sour and sallow and seldom left their mother's house. At Thanksgiving, she'd offered, in the most tactful way possible, to get him a deal on a place of his own. His response had been to upend his plate of turkey, mashed potatoes and gravy on her dining room table before throwing his wine glass against the wall.

They hadn't spoken since.

Thus, when she was assigned the listing of the house on Abigail Lane, Doug Lowell's story had a profound effect on her. She couldn't help but dread a similar fate for Graham. The light in his eyes had gone out and she felt powerless to protect him the way he'd sworn to protect her all those years ago. "Leave him be, he'll figure it out on his own," was her husband's advice, but that was his answer to everything, and in this case, ignoring the problem seemed like a terrible mistake. But what else was she to do?

With no easy answers, she distracted herself with research, and was intrigued by the information she uncovered. How, she wondered, had the house avoided closer scrutiny with all that had happened there over the years? She continued to dig, and thus, became the first person to connect the disappearances of Elmore Washington, Harold and Bud Wilson, the peculiar incidences of people and animals awaking to find themselves on the yard outside, and the Lowell family's abandonment of the house, even if the full scope of Doug's experiences hadn't yet been published. Had she not shown more interest in the house than was necessary to sell it, I doubt we'd know anything about it today.

A lifelong believer in the mystic, Sandy balked at her boss, Lou Terry's suggestion that she forget all she had learned, and countered that, while skeptics would be chased away by a house with a mysterious and possibly paranormal past, the more open-minded would love it, and might be willing to pay more than it was worth in the hope that they would experience something themselves. Though unconvinced, and unenthused by the idea of the property becoming a 'magnet for weirdos', Lou let her run with it.

Before submitting the listing to the customary venues, Sandy intended to write up a piece for *Fate* Magazine, but first, wanted to get a sense of the place herself. It's hard to know whether she genuinely *believed* there was something unnatural about the house, or if she just got a kick from the idea of selling it that way, but the article never happened. When the house eventually got sold, Sandy did not make the sale, because on the night of April 16th, 1975, she too vanished off the face of the earth. She'd argued with her husband Jack earlier. It would emerge in the subsequent investigation into her disappearance that the cause of that argument was her decision to return to the house after sharing with him what had happened three nights prior, an account he'd considered the first sign that maybe her big brother was not the only lunatic in the family.

"She came home on the night of the 12th in a frenzy. Manic in a way I'd never seen," Jack told reporters, and it's hard when you look at that news footage to not be repelled by the fame-hungry glint in his eye. A good actor, he was not, and his eagerness to be someone of note shines through despite the gravity of the situation. He was like a man who finds out his neighbor has won the lottery. He has no claim to it, but figures if he plays his cards right, he might end better off than he started. True to form, he milked the media attention from his wife's disappearance for the better part of a decade before dropping dead of a heart attack outside a movie theater in Chillicothe. He'd been waiting in line to see *Police Academy*. "But she wasn't scared," he said. "I mean, maybe a little. If anything, she was excited. Shaking. She had this look, like she'd...I dunno, seen God or something, or a magic trick."

Rather than test your patience with the rest of his rambling account, I'll summarize it for you here.

It was not God that Sandy Radcliffe saw that night in Number 56.

It was a lighthouse.

* * *

The power had not yet been turned back on. That wouldn't happen until the house was ready to show, so Sandy brought a flashlight. It was close to seven p.m., but at that time of year, the sun was a distant fire suffocating under the smoke of encroaching dark. She did not feel apprehensive as she made her way up the driveway to the house. Instead, she felt the first latent strands of the unbridled excitement Jack would see in full bloom later.

In truth, she did not expect to encounter anything mysterious inside Number 56, for while she believed in the supernatural, she had never directly encountered it, and this was, after all, not the first house she'd represented with a strange reputation. She recalled a previous client who'd sold his three-bedroom ranch over on Beaumont Street after claiming he could hear voices taunting him from the basement. Those voices turned out to be nothing more insidious than antiquated plumbing, which left her more curious about the man than the house. But that was always the way, wasn't it? Houses are empty shells of wood and brick and plaster, devoid of souls, or intent. It's us, the creatures that are installed within them, that ultimately define their character. Still, Sandy wanted there to be *something* inside that house, wanted to brush against the other side if only so she could continue to resist the idea that *this*, a finite and frequently cruel life, is all there is. Someday, perhaps sooner than she wished, her loved ones would die. Her father already had, and she desperately wanted to think of him as anything other than a cluster of bones buried in the cold uncaring earth. And if her brother didn't get the help he so desperately needed, his story would probably reach a premature conclusion too. She wanted to see them again, somewhere, somehow, wanted some sign that we go on.

As she stood on the stoop fishing through her keys, a soft light washed over her and then was gone. At first, she assumed it nothing more than the headlights of a car reflected in the living room window, but she hadn't heard an engine. Curious, she looked to her right, toward the deserted street, and a moment later the light flared again, drawing her attention back to the window once more. The blinds were partially open, and as she watched, the light flashed a third time, a glow from somewhere upstairs, as of a flashlight beam from inside one of the bedrooms. Sandy hesitated, ground the meat of her thumb over the ridges of the front door key. Was someone inside? It was hardly uncommon for vagrants to seek out unoccupied homes for shelter, a situation that had become significantly worse since the war. But how many vagrants carried flashlights? The possibility of a burglar seemed more likely, except that there was nothing inside left to steal. The notion of stripping copper wire from abandoned homes had not yet become the problem it would decades later, and even if it had, the house on Abigail Lane had been fitted with aluminum wire, though this substitute was problematic and would soon be phased out as an alternative.

Quietly, Sandy tested the front door and found it locked. Perhaps the interloper had admitted himself via the back door. She considered calling the police, or at the very least, running to her car and getting the hell out of there. She knew it was what a *sensible* person would do. And later, when a horrified Jack asked her why she hadn't, why she'd instead proceeded into the house, she gave him a queer smile, her eyes still filled with magic. Her response would become as integral a part of the house's story as the building itself: "It felt like it was calling to me."

Sandy opened the door.

Inside, she found only darkness in the empty living room, but cool blue light splashed against the wall at the top of the stairs in ten-second intervals. *Turn around*, she told herself. *He still doesn't know you're here.* But even as she counseled herself, she didn't believe it was a man or a burglar of any kind up there sweeping his light around. For one, such carelessness would not be typical of an intruder. No thief worth his salt would allow the light to be seen so clearly from outside the house. And for another, she still did not feel uneasy. Instead, that flutter in her belly had graduated to a steady hum of excitement in her bones. She sensed no danger here. What she sensed instead was the presence of...*something else*, something different.

Trembling, she crossed the room to the foot of the stairs and looked up.

Darkness.

In a whisper, she counted down from ten.

10...9...

Put one foot on the bottom step. It creaked beneath her weight.

...8...7...

She grabbed hold of the railing and pulled herself up another step. The darkness above remained unbroken, but now the hum she felt in her bones seemed to come from elsewhere, a wave of tangible distortion, like the tension in the air before a violent storm.

...6...5...

Another step and the hair prickled all over her body, like she was standing close to a power line. Breath held, she mounted the last two steps and stood at the top of the stairs, eyes wide, waiting.

...4...3...

In that moment she felt like she imagined the astronauts had as they took their first step down into the unknown. That was only six years ago and until it happened, nobody believed it possible. It sounded like madness, like talk of Atlantis and gods. A man on the moon? Preposterous.

...2...

And yet, by some miracle of science and physics, they'd done it, and now here she stood on the precipice of something equally unknown and terrifying and exciting and—

...1.

Brilliant light exploded in her eyes and turned the upstairs hallway white. She gasped and covered her eyes, but only for a moment, afraid that she might miss something.

The light passed. Sandy blinked to let her eyes adjust to the new dark, and as focus returned, her heart soared, her mouth popping open to allow the exit of a trembling awestruck breath.

She was standing near the edge of a cliff, the long grass blowing in a stiff breeze that carried to her the briny smell of the ocean below. Slowly, she shook her head to deny the reality of what she was seeing, even as the stars, each one binary, emerged from the darkness left in the wake of the light. The light flared again and she shut her eyes, convinced that when she opened them again, this place, this *otherwhere* would be gone and she would find herself once more standing on the landing of an ordinary house. The possibility of this filled her with inexplicable sadness.

But when she looked, it was still there. To her left, anchored atop a chaos of jagged rocks, stood an impossibly tall and narrow white column of stone. Around it, raged a troubled sea. From base to peak, the lighthouse was tattooed with dark symbols, jagged hieroglyphs, or perhaps it was just ivy or some other kind of creeping plant. Sandy did not know enough about vegetation to say whether it was even possible for it to grow here. *Here.* She uttered a small hysterical giggle. And where was *here*, exactly? Heaven? The Twilight Zone? The languid lighthouse beam found her, as if trying to scrub such foolish notions from her mind, and this time, as the brilliant light blazed into her, her head filled with the sound of old violin music played on scratched vinyl, a small connection to the real world, and then the beam and the music moved on. In its wake, Sandy, eyes filled with tears, fell to her knees. The long grass hissed against her legs. The air blew her hair around her face as she followed a new source a light over the cliff edge to her right, where she saw, perhaps 400 feet below, a long narrow stretch of beach, the cobalt-colored sand glowing as if in response to moonlight. But there was no moon, only a small lonesome bonfire, which, like the lighthouse, felt like a lantern in the night and a lure to her soul. At the far end of the beach, lofty cliffs rose up into the sky, their crowns studded with spindly limbed trees that swayed and whispered in the breeze. There was little to distinguish this place as otherworldly other than the fact that it was here, at the top of the stairs, and the sense deep inside her that if she spent the rest of her life traveling earthly coasts, she would never find its equal.

She looked back over her shoulder, expecting the house to be gone, expecting to see a continuation of this strange maritime plain behind her, but the stairs were still there, the living room an ordinary sight rendered alien by comparison to what she had seen and where she felt she belonged. She looked around the edges of this reality where it met the house but saw no seam, no demarcation where one became the other. The harder she tried, the more a headache started to drum itself up from the center of her skull—*Don't. Concern. Yourself. With. Such. Things*—so she stopped and looked back out from the lighthouse to her left, to the roiling sea ahead, and finally back to the bonfire down on the beach. The flames moved liquidly, as if time was different here, but the firelight spoke to her. It suggested that her presence in this place was just the start of something magical, that to truly begin her adventure, she must come to the fire, warm herself, and commit to what lay ahead.

And oh, how she wanted to. How she felt she must, that everything in her life from the turbulent to the quotidian had been a stepping stone to this moment, to this remarkable place. But what of her old life? What of Jack? As terrible as it seemed, in this face of this miracle, those things did not seem like compelling reasons to abandon her journey. Not that she would tell her husband that. Instead—

* * *

—she told him she walked home that night because she was so (elated) disturbed by what she had seen, she had not trusted herself to drive. This was mostly true, but it was designed to allow her an excuse to return, which she did, and that was the last anyone ever saw of her.

In the weeks after her disappearance, Jack speculated to the media that the whole thing was a hoax, that she was doing it all to raise the value of the house. He even applauded her gumption. But as the weeks turned to months, and it became clear he had seen the last of the woman to whom he'd been married for eleven years, he began to suspect she'd been having an affair and had simply run off, a suspicion aggravated by the discovery of Sandy's wedding ring on the second to last step of the stairs at Number 56. He held onto this story only until he realized he could profit from the paranormal angle, and then his beliefs changed again. The night she had come home so possessed by excitement, she told Jack all she had discovered about the house, the disappearances, the reports of animals and on that one memorable occasion, people, gathering in the lawn. She described for him what she had seen on the second-floor landing, the world that appeared there, all of which he thought was nonsense, and quite frankly, insane. But in later interviews, once he'd decided to cash in on Sandy's disappearance, he mentioned something he hadn't before, and to this day, it's unknown whether it was *actually* something she said, or just something he cobbled together to enhance the story. In the interview, he said the more he thought back on that night, the more certain he was that wherever his wife had gone, she'd gone there willingly, and he hoped wherever that place might be, that she was happy there. Then, he muttered something inaudible which the interviewer asked him to clarify. With a shrug, Jack repeated himself: "I said I hope she's happy in Valerine." He went on to explain that that was the name Sandy used for the place she had visited at the top of the stairs. At the time, he'd thought she said *Valentine*, until she said it again. When he asked her what that meant, she looked puzzled, as if she had no idea what he was talking about, as if it was her first time hearing the word.

Thus, the house claimed another soul.

At the time, the police had a less fantastical theory about what happened to Sandy Radcliffe but didn't have enough to make it stick. It's a theory that's been revisited ad nauseum in books, articles, podcasts and TV shows, despite ample evidence to the contrary.

They suspected her husband might have killed her.

VI

In a just world, a house connected to so many incidents would have been the subject of intense scrutiny by the police and the media, and yet, aside from each individual case and the investigations they merited, few people still seemed willing to look upon it as a culprit. Bad things happen all the time. People go missing for many reasons: depression, dissatisfaction with their lives or their spouses, money problems, a need to hide or start over. Humans are complicated creatures; houses are not. Still, once the Radcliffe case petered out, the house on Abigail Lane stood empty again for another four years. People might not have believed there was anything sinister or otherworldly about the place, but skepticism is always easier from a safe distance.

In that time, only two unusual incidents occurred, and those would not be uncovered until an author named Jay Anson wrote a book about an apparent haunting that made *another* house synonymous with the supernatural. The house was, of course, Amityville, and once Anson's book hit the bestseller lists in 1977, haunted places were suddenly a phenomenon worthy of global attention. By the time the movie adaptation scared the living hell out of audiences in 1979, armed with all manner of pseudoscientific equipment, self-proclaimed paranormal investigators and demonologists actively sought out alleged hauntings and made a respectable (and often absurd) living from books and articles written about their findings, few of which were ever independently verified, most likely because it was all fabricated. But nobody cared. Hauntings were big business. Hollywood ached to replicate the box office success of *The Amityville Horror*. Publishers wanted more bestselling books about bad places. And with Elvis Presley still fresh in the ground and Three-Mile Island serving as a reminder that any of us could wink out of existence at any minute, ghosts were in fashion.

Thus, when an article about the house on Abigail Lane appeared in *Odd Things*, a short-lived paranormal newsletter out of Bangor, Maine, one of the more prominent teams of paranormal investigators (if prominent is the proper word for ascendance in a field that relies almost entirely on not finding anything) took note.

Despite notable omissions and inaccuracies, the article in *Odd Things* was the first piece in print outlining the history of the house, from Elmore Washington to Sandy Radcliffe, and concluding with the two most recent events.

The first was neighbor Maggie Sundersen's claim that for four days straight, she could hear music coming from inside the house, a single song repeating on an endless loop, a song, she added, she used to love but now would never be able to hear again without feeling sick. It was "Dream a Little Dream of Me" by The Mamas and the Papas. After two sleepless nights, she reported it to the police, who arrived at the scene to absolute silence, only for the music to start up again once they were gone. Frustrated, Maggie asked her husband if he heard anything, but each time she brought it to someone's attention (the police, twice, three neighbors, and the mailman), the song stopped. Convinced someone was messing with her, she went to the door, but when she tried to knock, her fist plunged, not through wood, but some kind of gelid amber, honey-like substance. At the same time the music grew so loud (*"Say nighty-night and kiss me"*), Mary's ears began to bleed, and with all the strength she could muster, she yanked her hand free and ran screaming back to her house. The next day she sought out a doctor, who diagnosed her with tinnitus and advised her to avoid loud sounds, music especially, for the next few months. He didn't refer her to a psychiatrist, because he didn't believe a word of what she'd told him.

Jim Dancy the mailman, who'd been unable to corroborate Maggie's claims, had an experience of his own two months later.

"Three-thirty on a Friday," he said. "I never thought anything funny about the place. Never heard nothing, never saw nothing. I knew about those people going astray, but that happens, don't it? I don't believe in nothing but god himself and I ain't never seen no aliens or bigfeet or ghosts, just so you know I'm not some loon. And it was probably just somebody playing a trick on me. I don't know who'd do that. I know everyone on that street, even the kids, and I can't figure who might think it funny, but you know kids. They get strange notions. What I'd like to know is *how* they did it."

The "trick" to which he refers was the figure in the living room window looking out at him while he was placing a flyer for the new Korean restaurant The Jade Pearl into the mailbox. "Peeking at me through the curtains," he said. "Kid with a face like a stained and half-torn piece of yellow paper. He were dressed in a funeral suit, too. Upside-down he was, like he were standing on the damn ceiling. Now you tell me how someone, how a *kid*, could pull that off." It was probably for the best that Jim forgot that no curtains had hung in that window, or in any of the others at Number 56, for years. Jim continued, "I walked away, as you do when you're not sure what the hell you've just seen, but I looked back. I wish I hadn't, because there was another boy, or the same one, looking at me from the small window above the kitchen at the side of the house. I beat feet after that, because my momma didn't raise no fools, but I couldn't keep from thinking later that if I'd looked, I'd have seen the same thing in every one of those windows. But like I say, I guess it was just a prank, but I don't know why they'd want to scare an old man like that."

The Seekers were Julian and Julia Corman, an affable brother and sister team from Eau Claire, Wisconsin. Like many of the paranormal investigators who came before and after them, they used real science to distance themselves from the charlatanism so prevalent in the field. Here there were no crystal balls or Ouija boards or seances, only thermometers, VHS cameras equipped with jury-rigged thermal sensors, Geiger counters, and tape recorders. Neither of them would be standing in lightless rooms demanding the spooks show themselves, because the Cormans didn't believe the house was haunted, or at least, not by ghosts.

In her fascinating book, *Notes from the Other Side*, Julia writes: "I knew from the available facts that we weren't going to be facing restless ghosts or vengeful demons, or anything so outrageous. The house on Abigail Lane was not built upon an ancient burial ground or possessed by the spirits of the dead. One must always assume the dead have better things to do than exist just to pacify our fear of death. Everything we knew suggested a metaphysical aberration. We stepped over the threshold of an ordinary house in an ordinary neighborhood and over the threshold of modern knowledge. It is not a place steeped in old evil. It's a calamity of physics. There's a fissure, a gaping cosmic wound, a door to places we can't begin to fathom. Somehow, something we weren't meant to see is there in plain view, but only sometimes, and it's my theory that the door which opens at the top of the stairs was there before they built the house. It's probably been there longer than the earth. It was just dormant when they constructed the house around it, and now that house is like the building around an elevator, only we don't know which floor it will open onto at any given time, or what conditions it needs to do so."

Unlike many in their field, the Cormans were not out to exploit anyone for fame or personal gain. They were, like all the best scientists, curious, and wanted to try to understand how and why so many people had disappeared from the same place. The not-knowing maddened them, as did the lack of prior investigation, and they resolved to uncover the truth once and for all. They didn't, of course, not completely anyway, and it's unlikely anyone ever will, but along with the speculations of Arthur Windale and Patricia Burr, they ultimately contributed a great deal to our understanding of the Abigail House phenomenon.

"I'd like to think," Julia says in her book, "that the world into which my brother stepped that night was one in which he was welcome. On good days, when I recall the pair of crimson suns blazing above that field of sunflowers, I tell myself it was, but those days are rare, especially when I remember the tremor that shook us both, as of a colossal footfall, and then Julian's face when he turned to look at me. It was not the excitement that had been there a moment before, when the air at the top of the stairs seemed to pucker and then bow outward like a bubble, nor was it awe. It was horror, and then he was gone in the dark that rushed back in to seal the rift, a single incisor tumbling down the stairs behind him the only testimony that he'd been there at all. On my worst days, I think some manner of god stepped down from the sky into that field, but I can't bear to think of what it might have done to him. I pray I am wrong, or I pray it was quick. And to you, dear observer, I pray you don't judge me too harshly for what must sound like the diary of a madwoman. I grieve and thus cannot restrain my honesty. My whole life, my interest in all things has been scientific, but I find it difficult, in this instance, when reason is needed most, to apply it to what I've seen."

Julia Corman's book is not, as the title might suggest, about her experience with the paranormal, and only tangentially invokes the metaphysical. It's about mental health, specifically her battle with depression in the years following Julian's disappearance.

"I still wake up some nights and see him standing at the foot of my bed. I can't see his eyes, only his mouth. He is smiling at me in a way he never would, in a way I'd never have let him. What's worse is that I look too much like him to ever be able to escape the accusation I see in the mirror."

Julia's book went on to become a *New York Times* bestseller, lauded for its openness about un- and misdiagnosed medical disorders, grief, PTSD, and the stigma surrounding depression. In it, Julia admits to misleading the police when asked about the night's events not just because she knew the truth was too farfetched, but because she worried her mother would have her institutionalized, given Julia's history with bipolar disorder and her mother's tendency to either ignore or punish her for it. Meredith Corman held that mental illness was a convenient and overused excuse for weakness of character. Until her death from breast cancer in 2008, Julia worked tirelessly as a mental health advocate and women's rights activist. Director Mike Howard intended to feature a clip from *The Tonight Show with Jay Leno* from 2001 in which she discusses Abigail House, but his efforts were successfully blocked by her mother's attorney, who did not want to endure the embarrassment of having that old nonsense trotted out again.

Her legacy, however, extends far beyond the limits of this story.

VII

A few books were written about the house (among them Miles Dietrich's *Cursed House: My Encounter with Abigail*, Ghost Town Books, 1987), most of them nonfiction, blatant efforts to cash in on the still lucrative haunted house subgenre. One of the fictional efforts, *House of Death*, by Scott Tiller (Zebra Books, 1985), is trashy fun if you can detach yourself from the awfulness of the tragedies on which said fun is based, and the inexplicable cover illustration of a skeleton in a prom dress. Tiller at least had the decency to dedicate the book to the real-life victims he was exploiting. It was later turned into a terrible NBC TV movie called *Death House*, which aired only once before being buried, though some Internet sleuths have turned up the commercials for the film, which you can see on YouTube, assuming NBC/Universal haven't issued a takedown notice out of sheer embarrassment.

On June 5th, 1986, all the grass died in the yard outside Number 56. It had been fine, if too long and unruly, the evening before. Within a week, it turned completely black, as if it had been burned in a fire. Some say the house knew what was coming, but those are the same people who persist in ascribing the house a consciousness.

April 1987, and the new mailman, Bertrand Weems (Dancy retired a year after seeing the kid in the window), opens the mailbox at Number 56 to find it packed full of teeth, which rain down around his feet like ghoulish dice. They are later determined to be premolars from the mouths of horses. Weems did not bother to count them, but the police did. There were three hundred and sixty-seven of them. Like Jim Darcy before them, they deemed the incident a hoax, a morbid attempt to perpetuate the urban legends which had risen around Abigail House. They were summoned to the house again on Halloween night that same year, though this time the event was relatively normal. The neighbors had called them to report what appeared to be a coven of hooded figures encircling the house and chanting gibberish by candlelight. They fled at the sound of sirens, though three of them were apprehended. They claimed to be Satanists from The Church of Belial, their mission "to summon the demon from the hell beneath the house." They were freed without charge, though they would not be the last of their ilk to visit the house, for as much as Satanic Panic had parents throwing their kids' metal albums into the trash, there were those who saw catastrophic events like the murder of John Lennon, the advent of AIDS, the Challenger explosion, Chernobyl, and Black Monday, as signs of the impending apocalypse, and if God wasn't listening, maybe the devil would. After all, it's much easier to believe in Hell if you can already feel the flames.

On the 5th of September 1988, someone set fire to Abigail House. Authorities were alerted at three in the morning but arrived to find the conflagration had already burned itself out or had been put out. Bafflingly, the house remained undamaged but for extensive smoke staining on the exterior walls. Even the windows were intact. The arsonist, assuming there ever was one, was never apprehended.

February 1989. Researchers from OSU investigate the house at the request of the state. The investigation takes six weeks and is deemed "inconclusive".

In the footage from Mike Howard's documentary, researcher Shannon Hayes claims some of their findings were repressed by the university for fear of ridicule. "A prestigious institution could not be seen to endorse the radical beliefs of a small segment of the population to whom the paranormal is a viable substitute for logic," she explained. "We were there to disprove the claims of supernatural activity, not authenticate it."

When pressed by Howard to share some of what was removed from the report, Hayes is visibly uncomfortable.

"We were measuring temperature fluctuations and Dan [Moorehead], for no reason we could explain then or now, went blind in his right eye. He was on the third step of the stairs when he freaked out. I went to him and he shoved me away. 'Don't come up here," he said. 'Stay the [bleep] away, the air is wrong.' For eight months after that he claimed he saw things differently through that eye—*other places, another way*—and it made him happier than he had ever been in his life. But we examined him. There was a yellow cataract occluding his sight. There's no way he could have seen anything through it. He was legally blind in one eye. But he insisted we were wrong. He even refused surgery, rejected the idea of an intraocular lens. He said he didn't want to risk 'poisoning the view.' We were concerned it might be the result of a tumor, which would explain his inability to process the loss, but he seemed so [bleeping] happy, we quit trying to convince him he shouldn't be. Now of course, I wish we'd tried a little harder."

Dan Moorehead was found dead in his apartment in Hilliard on April 9th, 1989. He'd gouged out both his eyes with a meat fork and bled to death on the kitchen floor. Next to an uneaten breakfast of sausage, eggs, and bacon, was a note. It was one line, written in his own blood:

ALL HAIL THE SUNFLOWER GOD

It was declared another tragic suicide and Moorehead's name was omitted from the Abigail House report, before both were buried.

On May 12th, 1989, the doors and windows of the house were boarded up and NO TRESSPASSING signs were staked in the fallow yard. After thirty years of mystery, Abigail House was finally condemned.

That same night, a peculiar sound emerged from inside the house. It woke the neighbors and set dogs to howling. It didn't last long, but all who heard it recognized it for what it was. It was the sound of trees being felled in a dense wood.

Inside Number 56.

VIII

Arthur Windale noted that the 1990s represents the longest period of inactivity for the house, almost as if it was sulking, yet another example of people's tendency to anthropomorphize the place. But the house was never truly dormant. It would go weeks, even years without causing someone to blink out of existence, but that didn't mean other more innocuous things weren't happening, most of which probably went unnoticed by most, even as they were happening in plain view.

John Boone, who lived directly across the street from the house (much to his regret) woke one morning to the sound of incessant knocking and looked out the window. There was a man in a worn brown suit slamming a fist on the boards of the condemned house. "Let me in, you little peckerwood," he cried, over and over again. When this continued for the better part of an hour, John, who had tried and failed to keep to himself in a neighborhood gone to hell, got dressed and crossed the street to talk to the man.

"Hey, mister," he said. "Can I help you with something?"

The man spun around and was somehow still facing the door, still knocking, as if his whole body had rotated around inside itself only to return to its original position. John stopped dead at the curb, unsure of what he'd seen. The man continued to hammer on the boards. "LET. ME. *IN.*"

"Hey. Hey, man," John said again, a queasy feeling in his stomach. The air felt heavy and thin, and everything was somehow wrong.

Again, that bizarre optical illusion in which the man seemed to spin around to face him but didn't really move. It was as if there were two versions of the man and only one of them had turned to look while the other stayed facing the door. John felt sick and decided, whatever this was, it could be someone else's problem. "I'LL WRING YOUR GODDAMN NECK FOR FOULING UP MY PRECIOUS BABY. OH, YOU BETTER BET I WILL!" the man screamed then, and with one more knock, which sounded like a shotgun blast, he flickered from the door to John like a giant moth, and disappeared into a haze of yellow sparks and black dust.

John leaned over and retched onto the street.

He put his house on the market two days later.

* * *

On September 11th, 2001, when the Twin Towers fell, nobody came outside. Those who'd gone to work watched the horror on TV before being sent home.

The house had nothing to say.

* * *

By this time, those who believed there was something wrong with Number 56, who'd paid attention to the stories and verified them for themselves, also put their houses up for sale. Even if they thought it all so much blarney, they were tired of the frequent police visits, the media attention, the spook hunters and devil worshippers, the tourists and gawkers, the writers and would-be filmmakers. Their good neighborhood had gone bad. Others were simply annoyed at having a derelict house with a dead lawn bringing down the property values, and either complained incessantly to the housing authority, or started looking for someplace else to live. By 2004, of the twenty-three houses in the neighborhood, only fourteen were still occupied. The value of the remaining homes decreased by 40%, but by then, the happy couples who'd bought them in 1956 were too old and entrenched to move. Despite the economic growth under President Bush, Abigail Lane was dying. Whatever problems the residents had to that point, and there were many, they would soon grow worse as the Internet rose in popularity and people discovered that they could share their thoughts on anything with the whole world. Thus, while it sat there rotting, the mythos of Number 56 continued to build. It was a new era, one that would see the house become famous in a way it never had before. Obsession with the paranormal had never waned, but now ghost hunters had an unprecedented means of finding information and like-minded souls, and of organizing.

In the new millennium, secrets became harder to keep.

The house was about to go viral.

* * *

By the mid-2000s, the neighborhood was a poor sketch of its former self. Like many of its kind, in the half a century since its development as a place for young married couples, it had fallen to ruin. The asphalt was cracked. Trash gathered in the gutters. The streetlights were broken, and illicit activities conducted in the shadows.

In 2008, Arthur Windale started a blog entitled *The Things We Cannot Know*. He wrote about his various encounters and theories, including his visit to Abigail House. For reasons unknown, the post was picked up by news outlets and went viral. Social media exploded and for a week straight #TheAbigailPortal—the name of Windale's post—was among the top trending hashtags. Windale yet again found himself in high demand, and unsurprisingly, embraced it. He did the talk show circuit, announced he was in the process of putting together another book, and even began taking small groups of acolytes to the neighborhood, something the local police were less than happy about, but as it was more life than the neighborhood had seen in years, and seemed harmless enough, they relented. In his element, Windale held court on the street outside Number 56, ebulliently reiterating all the most soundbite-friendly parts of his blog post, to the delight of his rapt audience. The local news was there, covering the whole thing, though they must have found it all a little silly. Still, news was news.

Already buoyed by the renewed interest in his work, Windale could not have anticipated just how famous that night would make him. The ABC-affiliate's footage of the incident had, last time I looked, over 15 million views on Youtube.

Despite being made aware that he wouldn't, Windale's crowd were nevertheless disappointed that he didn't make an exception to his rule and give them a tour of the house, because from the outside, it looked no different than a hundred other abandoned homes in the suburbs. At least places like Amityville and the Winchester House had some sense of architectural grandeur about them. Abigail House just looked sad and defeated. Perhaps the interior might prove more interesting? But on this, Windale was immovable. He had studied the house enough to know that there truly was something off-kilter there. He believed everything he had read about the disappearances and had no doubt the house, or something inside it at least, had spirited those people away. He had no intention of putting his audience at risk to satisfy their curiosity.

As it turned out, he didn't need to give the people a tour, because that night, while he spoke on the street, a light began to pulse in the window behind him. It was initially dismissed as reflected glare from the television cameras or the audience's cell phones, all of which were raised in the air, but gradually people started to realize that it was coming from *inside* the house and that it had a pattern. Following the curious looks of the audience, who he'd noticed had ceased paying him much attention, Windale followed their gazes to the house in time to see the boards fall away from the front door as if pried off by invisible hands.

With a juddering moan, the door swung open and an old woman stepped out into the harsh white glow of the affiliate's cameras. "What have we here?" Windale is heard muttering on the video, and the excitement in his voice is clear. He has already realized the significance of the event. He couldn't take the people inside. In truth, he's afraid of the house, but by letting something *out*, it has given him a gift that will see him live out the rest of his years in prosperity.

If you watch the video, the woman's eyes are such a brilliant ethereal blue they penetrate even the lowest of resolutions. Her skin is dark brown, aged by the sun. She has a pair of small moles above her upper lip. Her head is shaved, and the dome of her skull patterned with intricate loops and swirls of dark ink. She wears wristlets of what appear to be fur, a necklace made of animal bones, and a smock made of tattered leather. It reaches to her knees. Her feet are bare and dirty. From the stoop, she looks around as if she's just woken up. Her searing blue eyes scan the crowd and Internet memes and viral videos are born of the moment in which she smiles. It is such a genuine, warm, and loving expression of pure joy it brings tears to the eyes of everyone who bears witness to it, even to this day. Like a figure from a dream, she fixes on Windale and walks across the dead lawn to him. Nobody on the street moves. They couldn't if they'd wanted to. They are in thrall to this woman now. That smile has possessed them, and they would rather die than not stay to see what happens next.

What happens is she stops before Arthur and takes his hand. Perplexed, fascinated, but unafraid, he watches as she places something into the palm of his hand and nods, her eyes moist. She closes his fingers and shakes his clenched fist up and down a few times, a silent acknowledgment of some kind. "What is this?" Windale asks, but she turns, casts the warmth of her gaze across the crowd one more time, and then walks away down the street until she is swallowed by the dark beneath the broken streetlights. The television crew attempts to follow, but somehow, in all the confusion, they lose her.

It was an interesting moment that would have faded quickly from the consciousness of all who saw it because in the end, as magnetic as she proved to be, the woman who came out of the house was still just some old woman, probably homeless, and therefore unconnected to the supernatural mystery which had drawn so much interest. There were even accusations that Windale had staged the whole thing.

In a follow-up video three days later, he silenced his critics and escalated the drama of the whole thing by holding two items up before the camera. One was the object the old woman had given him, a seashell no bigger than a plum, but unlike any shell seen on this earth. It was coal-black and striated with wavy lines of what one would assume to be silver. Depending on which way the shell is held, it gives out a soft sigh that sounds like the heaving of the sea. The genesis of that shell, initially suspected to be handmade, continues to elude modern science, because it's a composite of materials that, even on a molecular level, are alien. In his other hand, the somber-faced Windale held a large black and white photograph of a blonde woman, much younger than the one who appeared at the door of Number 56 on the night of the tour. Circled in red are the twin moles on her upper lip. They indeed appear to be the same person, separated by thirty years—Sandy Radcliffe.

Despite the immense intrigue generated by Sandy's reappearance, like all pop-culture phenomena and irresistible mysteries, the popularity and madness both on the Internet and off eventually forced it to collapse under its own weight, and people moved on to obsess over other things. There were those, like Windale, who were reluctant to let the legend of the place die without adequate explanation, and in the two years since Sandy Radcliffe's return, it's estimated that over thirteen more teams of paranormal investigators explored the house. Unless it remains undocumented, they did so without incident. To most, it became a footnote in the state's haunted history, a point of mild interest on the road to better attractions. The Discovery Channel announced a documentary about the house that never aired.

Windale continued to write his book, but perhaps fearing it might not be quite the literary juggernaut he'd once thought, decided to violate his own rule and enter the house in, he said, "the interest of more authentic coverage."

"Tomorrow," he wrote on his blog, "I'll be going alone into the belly of the beast in the hope that it will reveal itself to me. Stay tuned, my fine friends, for a tantalizing report as soon as I have one."

True to his word, he went inside Abigail House armed with only his cell phone, which he used only to record audio.

It was the last time anyone ever saw him.

The phone was found on the stairs. Following some terse descriptions of the interior, which he clearly meant to expound upon in his book ("squalid" "gloomy" "stinking of cat urine" "shameful symbol, fragility of the American dream") there comes a sound like a rusty metal door being forced or dragged open. Even on the recording, it's deafening. It's followed by a low roar, like a furnace, and when, three and a half minutes later, Windale speaks again, his voice is strained with amazement and fear.

"I asked for this. My God, I asked for it, didn't I? The answer? I don't know what I'm looking at. There's a warm draft though. It smells like smoke. And...I don't want to go up there. I don't want to, but I must, mustn't I?" His breathing is ragged, animalistic. There's the clomping sound of his boots on the stairs. One, two, three. Then he stops. "May as well be the face of God, and still they won't believe it. I'm not sure I believe it either and I'm looking at it. It's...it's a wall, black obsidian. I can't see where it starts or ends, but one edge of it is in view. There's...daylight, I think. Gray daylight. Or perhaps...I don't know...I don't know...impossible, look at it. There's a sound. Do you hear it? Like a flag fluttering in the breeze...Lord save me. It's enormous." Clomp, clomp, clomp, clomp. "Yes, a tower. A black tower, I think, leaning away at...at an angle...from...is that the sun or a fire...I can't tell. My God, it's so tall, and I'm up so high...The sound again." It indeed sounds like a flag snapping in the wind, but a moment later, Windale sees the source. "No, no. My God. My God. Not a flag at all. It's their wings. It's a host of—" Muffled thumps as the phone tumbles down the stairs and Windale is gone.

Those of a Christian bent have surmised that Windale was ferried to his maker on the wings of angels. There is no way to know that they are wrong. I'm an atheist and I prefer their version rather than think of that poor old man being sundered by devils in some hellish otherworld.

IX

Mike Howard had several short, critically acclaimed documentaries under his belt by the time he came upon the DON'T LOOK message board in August of 2015. As cyclical as the whims of the house, ghosts and grisly things were once again a hot commodity in Hollywood, and even those who specialized in nonfiction narratives were seeking to get in on it. It was Howard's agent Kassie Loomis who put him onto the message board, which she thought might be fertile ground for ideas. And she was right. Howard spent hours poring over the dozens of sub threads about Abigail House. He'd been eager to make something longer, a feature-length documentary, and even supposing a fraction of what he'd read on the message board had any basis in fact, he'd need that running time, or better yet, a series, in which to tell the story.

For eight months, he researched the house, bookmarking and printing off articles about the disappearances, the animal gatherings, the sleepwalkers, the sounds and the strange sights people had reported over the years. He made a list of the names involved and then checked to see if they were first, still alive, and second, willing to talk. He connected with Jeb Foreman's widow Martha, retired policeman and author Miles Dietrich, Alison Wilson, Sharon Grey's older brother Donald, Patricia Burr, Doug Lowell's daughter, Serena, author and clinical psychiatrist Karun Venkatesh, Sandy Radcliffe's brother George (contrary to her fears, he sought out the help he needed and ended up opening a successful hardware store in their home town), Cynthia Grant Stiles, former editor of *Odd Things*, Deputy Carson Sanders, Ohio State Police, neighbors Maggie Sunderson and John Boone, mailmen Jim Dancy and Bertrand Weems, OSU researcher Shannon Hayes, and dozens more.

Howard's intent was to create the most comprehensive record of the house's history to date, and in that, he succeeded. Much of what we know is due to his diligent efforts and painstaking research. He consulted with noted astrophysicists about magnetic fields, dark matter, and 'empty space'. In the film, he comes across as abrasive, argumentative. It's clear he isn't there to simply make the case that there was, from the beginning, something amiss with Abigail House. He wants to know *why*, and his tone demands the subjects, and the world, provide him with the answer. One of the more amusing segments in the documentary is his discussion with field geologist Irwin Cordwell about the land atop which the house was built. If Howard's hope was that Cordwell would reveal that the site was cursed, he was disappointed. Instead, the geologist told him a local news item from 1918 in which a farmer decries the ongoing theft of his livestock. The field from which the animals were snatched would, thirty-six years later, end up in the hands of Diamond & Halliwell Construction, who used it as the foundation for some of the houses in Abigail Lane, among them, Number 56.

Howard found the history of the house credible enough to be wary, but that didn't keep him from finding a way to keep an eye on it. Working alone so as not to put others at risk, he cordoned off the stairs and installed in the house three closed circuit cameras, one of which was angled to monitor the inside of the front door. The second was affixed to the living room ceiling and directed toward the stairs. The third was mounted as close to the stairwell as he dared get. "I'll do almost anything for my art except vanish into another dimension," he says with a smirk. "Unless the critics are kinder over there." Because there was no power in the house, he had to rely on battery packs, which required swapping out every few days, but they enabled him to view the house remotely, ensuring not only his own safety but that of everyone on his team. Every day for fourteen months, his crew worked in shifts so that someone was always watching the house from the monitors in Howard's apartment, but other than periods of distortion and specks of dancing light, they saw nothing of note.

The lack of a compelling result frustrated Howard. He knew it had been a long shot given the number of dormant periods in the house's recorded history, but he'd banked on seeing *something*. It was how he'd planned to end the film. The big shock at the end that would jolt viewers out of their disbelief.

His disappointment made him a tyrant. Three of his four team members quit, tired of his outbursts and ego. Only his girlfriend Therese stayed on board. She believed in him, and his film, and told him so in the hope of talking him down, but it was too late. Howard was already doomed. His anger and ambition made him incautious, and on the night of September 16th, 2018, he went back to the house either to retrieve or reposition the cameras, while Therese watched from home.

From her interview with *The Hollywood Reporter*:

"I didn't believe in the paranormal, or whatever Mike thought was going on. I'm a realist. I don't believe houses can erase people, or eat them, or whatever. But Mike did and I knew whatever the reason was for what people thought happened in that house, he would wring an amazing film out of it. It was just what he did, okay? He lived to find the truth behind things, to expose the dark holes in the world. And I didn't tell him not to go back to that house that night for a couple of reasons. Like, he'd been there dozens of times already and nothing had happened to him, so why would I try to stop him? All these people online calling me all sorts of names, blaming me for not being a better girlfriend, telling me I could have saved him. They don't know. I get harassed every day. Somebody even posted my address, okay, and I had to move. But it wasn't my fault. It wasn't. I didn't see the house the way he did. I just saw the film. And he wouldn't have listened to me anyway. Don't get me wrong. He listened to me all the time, just not when he needed to do something for the film, and I thought he should take a different approach. With his work, it was his way or no way at all, and I think instead of harassing me, people should respect his position and the position it put *me* in."

The interviewer asks what Therese saw on the monitors that night.

"I saw him enter the house. It was dark and the picture kept bowing in and out like it was struggling to focus or something. Right away I knew something was wrong, because I'd watched him do this dozens of times before. It was always the same process. He never hung around longer than he needed to because he didn't trust the place. He'd just go inside, take a quick look toward the stairs, swap out the batteries and then get the hell out of there. That night though, he stared at the stairs for so long, I checked to make sure the picture hadn't frozen, but I could see dust moving past the lens. And still Mike kept looking. At one point he shook his head like he was answering a question or something, and then he turned and looked up at me. He looked like a ghost. I knew he was looking at me, the only other person there with him. He looked up and he mouthed something. We know what he said now of course, but at the time, I found myself shaking my head and raising my hands as if he could see me. Then he pointed toward the stairs.

"I didn't understand what I was seeing, but for the first time I wondered if this was part of his plan, if he'd pulled the wool over all our eyes, because it looked like he'd installed a big video screen at the top of the stairs. How else to explain what I was seeing? All those images. All those people and places."

The interviewer asks her to detail some of those images.

"I saw a field crowded with sunflowers, so bright and pretty until something enormous moved in front of the sun and then the image changed, and I saw a lighthouse sweeping its beam over the sea. And then I saw a swimming pool full of fish, a small dusty room with a creepy clown snapping his claws at the audience, who laughed like he was the funniest thing they'd ever seen, a black rock or sharp mountain poking up at a sky full of huge birds; a field full of blind, grazing cows, a movie theater full of mannequins all facing us and not the screen, a big garage filled with cars that looked like they were made of metal, meat, and bone, a river of red roses, a bunch of kids looking out windows. It went on and on and on, a hundred scenes, maybe more, but instead of watching them all, I looked at Mike for explanation. He mouthed the same thing up at me again, desperation in his eyes, and again I shook my head. Eerily, he did the same, then smiled, and this time I did make out his words, though they were not the same ones as before: *I love you.*

"With dread in my heart I watched him walk out of one frame and into another, and on those monitors I saw him mount the stairs. I thought he might be going up to remove the video screen, but the way he'd said he loved me and the look on his face told me something was wrong. And it was, because he didn't remove the screen. Like everybody else, you'll tell me I'm crazy, and probably mock me like TMZ did, but I swear on my life, he *didn't* remove the screen, because it wasn't a screen at all. Whatever it was showed a desert full of ancient ruins, each one topped with black spires. Towering over them all was a stone statue of a giant. Its face was nothing but eyes, and its hands were colossal trees. More spires poked like black needles from the sand around its feet. I watched in disbelief, still sure this would turn out to be part of a clever hoax, as Mike stepped *through* the screen and then he was part of it. Inside it, somehow. The sand rolled away ahead of him as if something was alive beneath it, or as if his presence had caused a kind of shockwave. That's when I knew this was no illusion. He had time to look up at the camera one last time before the screen, the door, the whatever it was, snapped shut behind him, and I ran, ran, ran down my stairs to my car to go save him. But he was gone."

And what, asks the interviewer—who, like the rest of us, already knew thanks to the lipreader who decoded it the day it was made public—did he say to the camera before he disappeared?

"He said 'I think it's a door into someone else's dreams.'"

The documentary remains unfinished, but in an effort to try to draw Mike out of wherever he might be hiding, or in the hope that somebody might see it and come forward with information that might help locate him, Therese made the footage available for download on the Internet.

Which is where Scott Walker saw it.

X

On the 6th of September, 2018, Scott Walker returned from a meeting with his agent in New York. It had gone well. He'd signed a three-book deal with HarperCollins, which meant he'd get to breathe for a few days before sequestering himself in his office for the better part of three years. Scott was tired, ready to do nothing but vegetate in front of the TV, but that rarely happened anymore. As the saying in publishing goes, a writer is always writing, even when he's not.

His sixteen-year-old daughter Zoe was at the kitchen counter, an untouched plate full of her mother's vegetarian spaghetti and meatballs next to her. She was, as always, glued to her laptop.

"Hi, honey," he said, and kissed the top of her head.

"Dad," she said, hands aflutter. "You have *got* to watch this."

Scott loved his daughter dearly but confessed to not understanding her fascination with morbid stuff. Every week she tried to force him to watch another true crime documentary on Netflix, or worse, listen to some podcast in which nasally amateur sleuths rehashed facts that were freely available in books written decades before. He might have considered having a talk with her about the value of those shows that night, but as his wife had pointed out, he'd lost his vetting rights the minute he started writing horror stories.

Scott went to get a beer from the fridge. "What is it? More of those Vine things?"

"No, no. It's about a house not far from here. Just off Sawmill, I think? I dunno. It's somewhere close. Anyway, it's supposed to be, like, an urban legend or something because for years people have been disappearing there."

Scott cracked open the beer, took a long slug. "Oh yeah?"

"Yeah, they were making a documentary about it and there's footage of the director, like, getting sucked into some kind of portal or something. Come, see." To pacify her, he did, but was too wiped out to pay much attention to the grainy camera footage. So instead he kissed her once more and headed for the stairs. "Mom asleep?"

"Bridge night with Donny and Lo," she said.

"Ah, that's right. Well, I'll say goodnight now, then."

"Goodnight, and my name's not Nowthen."

"Hardy-har."

He showered and went to bed.

Zoe recalls she heard him screaming that night, but when she quizzed him the following morning, he pleaded ignorance. He was, however, unusually eager to see the video she had tried to show him the night before. He replayed the video so many times, she had to beg him to stop.

What follows was retrieved from the NOTES app on Scott's phone after it was retrieved in a field twenty miles south of Columbus:

The video was called "Mike Howard documentary SFX." Later, once I went back to the start of all of this and caught up to where Mike's documentary footage left it, I'd realize that this video was uploaded by another user, who edited it to show only Mike's last night in the house. But at the time, that was all I needed to see, and once I watched it, I sat back in the chair and tried to make sense of it all.

It isn't possible to remember every dream you've ever had, but most people remember some of them. I can only recall a handful of my most vivid dreams, or nightmares, many of them from my childhood.

All of them are in Mike Howard's video footage, playing on the screen at the top of the stairs.

After that night, I put my book on hold and spent all my time researching the house. I wanted to know how it was possible that over the course of sixty years, several people in the real world somehow walked into my dreams and nightmares, brought to vivid life by an unnatural house. I should have let it go, because the nature of the situation suggested it might drive me mad. Certainly, it was insane to expect a logical explanation. In the end I decided I must not have had those dreams after all. A more likely explanation was that I saw the Howard video somewhere, or came across an article, maybe that old guy Windale's blog, and my mind created false memories from the fragments.

But I know this isn't true.

When I was seven years old, I woke up screaming so loudly my mother ran into the room to comfort me because I'd dreamed of a clown that had insectile limbs and cockroaches crawling under his shirt. Even when I woke, I thought he was inside the room, but it was just my Abominable Snowman onesie hanging in the closet. My stepfather was less kind about it. For weeks, right before my bedtime, he'd jump out at me from under the stairs, hands raised to his face, fingers wiggling, and cry out: "CLOWNMANTIS, LIVE IN FIVE!" and get great pleasure from my fear.

When I was fourteen, I almost choked in my sleep while dreaming of an alien planet presided over by a stone god who had stolen all the air and sent needles up through the sand to impale explorers. I had read Frank Herbert's *Dune* only three weeks prior.

I know when I first fell in love, I dreamed of the kind of place where we wouldn't have to go to school, or work for a living, or deal with grownups. I dreamed we were marooned on a distant island lit by a towering lighthouse. There, we would live off the land and be together until the stars burned out. I was young, and silly, a hopeless and clueless romantic. In school, I fantasized about that place. I saw us there, me and Ramona. I even christened the place Valerine after a character from one of my favorite fantasy novels. And I know when she broke up with me, I had nightmares about her asshole father coming to my door to make me answer for trying to talk his daughter into sleeping with me. I dreamed of going to her house and begging her to give me another chance, but she wouldn't come to the door. Her brother Liam, that irritating little shit, was in every window, watching.

All the alleged horrors that befell the people who disappeared in Abigail House were taken from inside my head, but how? I wasn't born until 1971. HOW then, did my dreams manifest themselves back in 1956? One theory is that the dreams preceded my mind's screening of them, as if after I was born my brain became an antenna that picked up transmissions from somewhere else. But where? Deep space? Another dimension?

If you're looking for a concrete answer, you're going to be disappointed, just as I was yesterday when I went to see the empty lot where the house once stood. I thought it might spark something in me, trigger some grand revelation that would make sense of everything, but it didn't. I will die never knowing how or why any of this happened to me, and to others.

All I got from that visit was a headache from the smell of engine oil.

* * *

No. No, I was wrong. Oh God, I was so very wrong. The house...the door...it was there all along...

...I went home, to what I *thought* was my home. At first, I didn't notice the differences. Zoe was there at the counter. God. Her face. No eyes. No eyes. My wife, in the shower, scales on her back. I ran, God forgive me, I ran and—

* * *

i'm sorry to my wife and daughter there was not supposed to be an ending not supposed to ask questions for which there are no answers but i did i didn't know i'm sorry to the lost and wonder where you are i am no longer there and i'm sorry you got lost in my dreams

my head hurts I am here now and I have found my faith and it smells like clay

the old world is gone
only the field and the flowers
and the one who put them there
he has promised to teach me
i have
promised to
listen
if i listen
everything

will be okay
all hail
the
sunflower
god

*　*　*

As of yesterday, the neighborhood of Abigail Lane is no more. Nothing remains of the houses which once stood there but the memories. Trucks and construction crews have come and gone, and the land has been leveled and sold. The cheery billboard out front shows a family staring up in awe at a massive futuristic mall. Beneath it, is a date: June 2026.

WE LIVE INSIDE YOUR EYES (II)

CHARLIE RISES FROM THE FLOOR. The notebook bearing the title "The House on Abigail Lane" falls to the floor and turns to ash, just like all the others. He sees everything so clearly now. The ivy binding the woman to the pillar snaps and falls away, and she steps down into the ring of light before him. All of this he watches through eyes that are both new and ancient at the same time.

"You are ready now," the girl says from somewhere, from everywhere in the room. "You have outgrown this old dead world and these old dead souls. Those stories are doors to other realms. Go and see them. Spread the word of The Bone Mother. Spread the word of the Stone Gods, for they shall be coming soon."

"Yes," Charlie says, as The Bone Mother removes her mask and he is bathed in the glory of her regard. She has universes for eyes and mountains for teeth. "Yes," he says and weeps with joy, as her hands find his shoulders and her cold hard fingers reach for his mouth.

"Yes," he wails in ecstasy before she frees him from his tongue.

Night comes and he lets the girl and The Bone Mother guide him out of the ruins. He scarcely notices the houses have collapsed into sodden ruin, and would hardly have cared if he had. He steps over the pulverized bodies of The Cruel Boys with nary a second glance. They, like everything else in this world, are meaningless.

Together they walk to the edge of the neighborhood, to the edge of the world, where they gaze into the lightless abyss, inside which, other worlds hide in the dark, praying to escape the attention of gods, even as the gods look back, eager to open those worlds like volumes in an ancient library.

STORY NOTES

"The Land of Sunshine"

My brother was an art and design student in college when this story was conceived. One night, while we were chatting on Skype, he mentioned that he needed a story for a Claymation project that was due in a few weeks' time. Immediately I envisioned crooked buildings and murky nightscapes, real Tim Burton stuff, which I thought would be both fun and challenging for my brother to realize. I mentioned to him that I had the seedling of an idea about a man who must traverse a nightmarish cityscape in search of his own heart, and he was intrigued. However, as is frequently the case with me, other business got in the way, and by the time I managed to get the story written, the deadline for his project had come and gone and he had already submitted something else. Happily, he wasn't inconvenienced, and my procrastination did not have an adverse impact on his grades. He later graduated, and this wayward story ended up finding a dark and welcoming home of its own.

"Traveler"

Is there anything more frightening than the idea of losing your identity, of feeling as if someone else has occupied and taken control of your body? Can you imagine waking up with no recollection of what you've done only to discover that it's something catastrophic? Imagine having to answer for a crime you don't remember committing. Such questions inspired this story, as well as a dash of one of my favorite plays, *Death and the Maiden* by Ariel Dorfman, about deceit, paranoia, and the malleability of truth under duress.

"The Mannequin Challenge"

You may remember, back in November 2016, social media timelines became host to a series of videos in which people pretended to be frozen while a camera moved around them. Kind of like adults playing Simon Says. The more popular and widespread these so-called 'Mannequin Challenges' got, the more elaborate and star-studded they became. Everyone wanted in on them. But while it was fun to see how clever and inventive people could get with the concept, I couldn't help wondering what would happen if someone who didn't know what was happening, and who had never even *heard* of these orchestrated challenges, encountered one *in media res*. Add in a soupçon of bitterness and office politics and you have the genesis of this nasty little tale.

"Go Warily After Dark"

I haven't written many war stories. In fact, I think this might be my only one to date, and it deals less with the conflict than the collateral damage on the citizens of the unnamed city. If it feels like I'm writing about the bombing of London during World War II here, that's intentional. I was reading about life during that horrendous period and came upon a mention of the warning posters which advised the citizens to be mindful of curfew, specifically to "go warily after dark." Those words summoned this story because as we all know, and history is quick to remind us, evil thrives in darkness, and the world is never darker than during times of war.

"Down Here with Us"

Another first. This was written for a shared-world horror/fantasy anthology, *Tales of the Lost Citadel*, and if I hadn't been invited to contribute, I doubt I'd ever have written a story quite like it. And while I was a little intimidated at the idea of straying so far outside my comfort zone, I thoroughly enjoyed writing about these once-proud warriors, now little more than slaves in a rapidly disintegrating world.

"Sanctuary"

I write about kids and imagination a lot, probably because my childhood was marked as much by magic as darkness and so those themes keep coming back to me. Written for an anthology about cities, the place in which this story is set is based, not on a city at all, but a village in Ireland where I spent much of my childhood. My grandparents lived there, and I did, on occasion, have to fetch my grandfather from the pub on cold afternoons. Everything about my memories of those days and that place is benevolent and happy, however, so naturally I had to warp the hell out of them for this story. That is, after all, what I do.

"A Wicked Thirst"

One night, after drinking three days straight, I woke up face down in a puddle in an unfamiliar neighborhood. I was immediately confused, then terrified, and even though I had GPS on my phone, it never occurred to me to use it. I could have been a hundred miles from home, and it was not the first time I'd found myself in such a miserable state. Shirtless and freezing, I ran to the porch of one of the dark houses where I'd spied an Amazon box, cadged the address, and called a cab. Imagine my embarrassment when the surly driver took a right turn, then one more, and dropped me off outside my house. I'd been less than three minutes' walk from my house, but in my confusion had staggered into the adjacent neighborhood. It's funny now, but it wasn't then, and it led to me having a long conversation with myself about my tendency to abuse alcohol. As part of the process, I wrote this story.

"The No One: A Rhyme"

Last year, for no good reason at all, I found myself compelled to write poetry. I would be lying on the couch watching TV when a stanza of verse would pop into my head and I would have to write it down. Soon this was happening almost every night, usually late, and by the time I was done, I had half a book of poetry saved in my files. This might not be so odd but for the fact that I don't *write* poetry. Oh, there's been an occasional verse here and there, but none of it has been any good. For a time, I considered gathering up these poems, many of them written in the throes of depression, and making a book of them, but the more I read back over them, the less connected to them I felt. Thus, they remain filed away for review sometime in the future. But for this book, I chose the one I liked the best, the one that reads like it was meant to survive, one that even poetry haters could appreciate, and included it for you here.

"You Have Nothing to Fear from Me"

I don't have a lot to say about this one that won't be obvious from the story, or the news. I've known a lot of women in my life, and every single one of them had scars, mental, physical, or both, given to them by men they trusted and loved. I've caused some scars too. Any man who claims different is hiding the truth from himself.

And whether they were intentional or not doesn't change the fact that this has always been a tough world for women, and we have not done enough to change that.

"The Monster Under the Bed"

Sometimes, just for kicks, I write small dialogue-only stories and post them on social media. There's not much to them. No depth, character development, or scene setting. Thus, there's not much to say about them, here or anywhere else. But who among you doesn't love a good comeuppance piece?

"The House on Abigail Lane"

There are over a million words of unfinished stories in my files. Over a *million*. Most of it will never be seen by human eyes, but every now and again I'll go in and have a peek at what's there. Among the corpses are a handful of aborted novels, including over fifty pages of a *Kin* sequel. There's a kaiju novella, abandoned twenty pages from the end because of its similarity to a popular horror novel that was released while I was writing it, and a novel about paintings that come to life that I ditched after watching *Velvet Buzzsaw*. Stories can die for all kinds of reasons. Sometimes you lose steam, sometimes you get stuck, sometimes someone else gets to the idea first, and sometimes the excitement for a project wanes and you jump to a horse with sturdier legs.

During one of these expeditions into The Crypt, I chanced upon a single page of a story I'd started three or four years ago about a house in which people vanish when they go upstairs. There was enough on the page to intrigue me, and I really liked the tone of it. It had a true-crime-y feel, and when I reached the end of that page, I found myself eager to know what happened next. So, I took it out, dusted it off, rewrote that first page and the story caught fire. I hope its reanimated corpse entertained you.

We Live Inside Your Eyes (I & II)

When I was a kid, I spent a lot of time in my bedroom looking out the window. Eleanor, the girl in the house across the street, used to do the same, and we would signal to each other for hours. This graduated to walking to school together, and later, she was my first kiss. This story is my affectionate nod to those simple, exciting, confusing times, and an expression of my gratitude that she resisted the urge to sacrifice me to The Bone Mother.

ABOUT THE AUTHOR

KEALAN PATRICK BURKE is the Bram Stoker Award-winning author of six novels, numerous collections, and over two hundred short stories. He has no spare time, but if he did, he'd probably use it to do a bunch of things he wouldn't want to talk about. Or play videogames and junk, whichever required the least amount of effort. Visit him on the web at www.kealanpatrickburke.com or on Twitter @kealanburke, where he (thinks he) is hilarious.

Printed in Great Britain
by Amazon